On
Winter's
Wind

On Winter's Wind

A Novel by Patricia Hermes

Little, Brown and Company

BOSTON   NEW YORK   TORONTO   LONDON

First Edition

This novel is a work of fiction. Names, characters, places, and incidents are either the product of the author's imagination or, if real, are used fictitiously.

Library of Congress Cataloging-in-Publication Data

Hermes, Patricia.
    On winter's wind / a novel by Patricia Hermes. — 1st ed.
        p.   cm.
    Summary: As she struggles to make ends meet while maintaining her family's dignity, eleven-year-old Genevieve faces the possibility of turning in a slave for the bounty.
    ISBN 0-316-35978-5
    [1. Fugitive slaves — Fiction. 2. Slavery — Fiction. 3. Afro-Americans — Fiction. 4. Conduct of life — Fiction. 5. Family life — Fiction.]   I. Title.
    PZ7.H43170n   1995
    [Fic] — dc20   95-13840

10   9   8   7   6   5   4   3   2   1
HC

Published simultaneously in Canada by Little, Brown & Company (Canada) Limited and in Great Britain by Little, Brown and Company (UK) Limited
Printed in the United States of America

For my friend Frank Hodge

and

In memory of my friend Bill Braster

On Winter's Wind

∼ Chapter One ∽

I sat beside Leila on the bottom step of the long hall stairway, her head against my shoulder. I kept looking down at her, then away into the darkness, then back, wondering if she was ready to go up to bed. She didn't seem to notice me looking, though, or else pretended not to. She sat quietly, cuddled against me, occasionally fiddling with a string she had pulled from the edge of the carpet and wound around one finger. Every little while, she'd pull away from me and sit up straight, her head tilted to one side, that way she has of listening. Then she'd sigh and settle against my side again.

The grandfather clock at the far end of the hall struck once, the chime loud in the dark hall. After a minute, the sound faded, the echo dying slowly.

Was it one o'clock, or half past twelve? The midnight chimes had rung some while ago, but from here, with only the candle, it was too dark to see the face of the clock.

I remembered what Leila had said the last time we'd been here when the midnight chimes rang — that sounds had little lives of their own, that they floated up in the darkness like soap bubbles, drifting higher and higher till they bumped against the ceiling and were no longer bubbles or sounds, but nothing. Gone. Alive for a moment and then all gone! She'd thrown her arms out wide, just the way she'd done when she was a little baby.

I hugged myself tight, shivering. It was too dark to see the ceiling now — or sounds, either, if I could really imagine them floating like that. But I could picture the ceiling in my mind's eye: a deep midnight blue, pinpointed with tiny dots of white and silver. Stars on a night sky, it's supposed to be, an indoor sky. Papa had an artist paint it for Leila and me before he went away last time, three years ago, when I was just eight and Leila five, not much more than a baby. Papa said the sky would remind us of him out there at sea, that we could look at our painted sky, just as he watched God's sky. We would think of each other that way until he came home, he said.

I thought of him practically all the time now. And from these nights on the stairs, I knew Leila did, too.

It was to be a short trip, Papa had promised, a year or two at most, maybe his last one to sea, the last needed to secure his wealth — our wealth, Mama had said proudly.

I looked down at Leila again. She was really still, breathing softly, her head heavy against my arm.

"Leila?" I whispered. "Are you awake?"

"Hmm," she murmured.

"Are you cold?" I asked.

She nodded. "A little. But you keep me warm."

I had to smile at that. Keep her warm? I was freezing! But her head did feel warm where it lay against my arm.

"Come, Leila," I said softly. "It's foolish to be sitting here in the middle of the night. You're not going to hear anything tonight. Let's go to bed."

"You can go, Genevieve," she said, looking up at me. "I don't care about waiting alone."

As she looked at me, the candle threw soft shadows on her face, on her huge brown eyes and the hollows around them, her hair so long in front it almost covered her eyebrows.

Leila is tiny, smaller than other girls her age, and so thin I can circle her wrist with the thumb and forefinger of one hand. She reminds me of a bird sometimes, that baby bird I saw last spring that had fallen from its nest, its bones so tiny it was hard to believe they were bones at all. But even though she's so frail-looking, surprisingly she's hardly ever sick. Still, I worried about her, especially because lately there'd been so little decent food in the house to eat. Both she and I were going hungry many days, trying to leave extra food for Mama, or trying to leave some so there'd be enough for the next meal, yet Leila never complained. It was hard because the money Papa had saved for us, money to see us through the time he was gone, had run out. Yet even though being hungry was unpleasant, it wasn't the worst part of our lives these days. The worst was that Mama pretended nothing had changed, that we were still wealthy, pretended not to even notice how hungry and cold we were. I knew it was hard for her, yet I wished she would let me do something to help. I sighed, thinking of her, remembering what she says when I suggest a plan to help ourselves: "God will provide."

"Gen?" Leila said now. "Is something wrong?"

"No," I said. "Why?"

"You can go to bed," she said. "Really. I mean it. I don't mind the least bit if you go to bed."

"I know you don't mind," I said, "but I do! I'm not leaving you to freeze here alone. Now, come on. It's half past twelve at least."

"One o'clock," she said.

I glared at her. "One o'clock, then!" I said. "And there's school tomorrow."

She looked away and twisted that bit of string. "But I'm listening," she said softly.

"Well, listen upstairs in bed!" I answered.

She looked up at me. "This is where the sea sounds come!" she said, as if I didn't know that. "As soon as the ship comes near enough, we'll hear it, if we stay here. Do listen!"

She held up a hand and leaned her head to the side. "Hear that?" she said. "Hear the waves?"

I rolled my eyes and didn't answer.

Of course I heard the waves. But that didn't mean we'd hear a ship.

And I didn't have to listen, anyway. I knew, just as she did, about the strange way that sea sounds travel, here and outside, too. Outside, I can stand on Carpenter's Hill, high above the ocean, looking right down to the water, and can hardly hear the pounding of the waves. But then, walk up to Market Street, where the stores are and where the bounty hunters have posted their signs, much farther inland, and I can hear sea sounds all around, as though waves are crashing right at my feet.

It's like that in this house. In certain rooms, before I went about shutting down all but four of the rooms to save heat in spite of Mama's protests, there are no sounds of the sea. Here on the stairs, though, where Leila and I were sitting, one can hear everything — the roaring, pounding surf in winter storms, the humming and sighing of the waves on quiet nights like this one. During huge storms, it even sometimes seems as though waves are lapping at the foot of our porch, wanting to devour it and carry it out to sea.

The sea sounds aren't the important thing, though. It's the ship sounds. Leila was listening once again for ship sounds, sounds that travel better at night, she says, when most living things are sleeping.

Leila hears things, whisperings from the sea, dream messages, things that ordinary people don't hear or know. Sometimes I get angry with her, because I think she imagines those things, makes them up to make herself seem important. But then sometimes she's right, like the time she predicted a hurricane that no one else had predicted, not even the sailors who know and read the seas and skies and winds. That time, Papa delayed his sailing for one whole week because he believed her. It saved his ship and men. It maybe even saved his life.

I sat up straighter, still hugging myself to get warm. "You're being very annoying," I said. "It will worry Mama half to death if she finds out how late we were up."

Leila looked up at me. Even in the near dark, I could see her impish grin. "Who will tell her?" she said.

"I will!" I said. Although of course I wouldn't.

"Will not!" Leila said, laughing.

There was a long silence, and then she added quietly, "I just want to hear something, Gen. I know if we wait long enough, I'll hear the ship."

I didn't answer, because we had had this argument many, many times before, and I didn't believe at all that there was a ship coming. Not the ship she was hoping for, anyway.

I sighed, and Leila did, too.

She stood up. "All right," she said. "I'm coming."

"Good!" I said.

I didn't ask why the change of heart, unless she was just as cold and tired as I was.

I picked up the hem of my dressing gown. Then I held the candle high so Leila could see, too, and together we tiptoed up the stairs, being careful to avoid the creaking step second from the top.

When we were in our room, Leila snatched her angel doll off the bedside stand and took a flying leap into bed.

By the time I had doused the candle and taken off my dressing gown, Leila's breathing was soft and calm, as though she were already off in sleep.

But as I crept in beside her, snuggling in close, rump to rump for warmth, she spoke. "Tomorrow, Genevieve," she whispered. "We'll hear the ship tomorrow."

❧ Chapter Two ❧

Next morning, I left Leila in bed asleep, her arms wrapped tight around her pillow, her little face calm, her breathing soft and sweet. Watching her resting so peacefully, knowing how little sleep she'd had, I couldn't bear to wake her. So I left a note for Mama on the hall table, telling her that Leila was still in bed and that I thought she needed rest — hoping Leila wouldn't be angry with me, since I know how she loves school.

I went downstairs then. There wasn't much in the pantry, but there was a loaf of bread and some lard, so I made myself two lard sandwiches. I ate one and put the other in my lunch pail. Then I put on my coat, picked up my books and lunch pail, and went out the back way, across the alley to Sarah's house. Our houses are right next door to each other's, and we always meet back there to walk to school or, in summertime, to play or tell secrets.

Sarah wasn't outside yet, so I waited, standing sheltered in the outcropping of her father's stables, my shoulders hunched, my hands pulled up inside my sleeves. It had begun to snow, and the wind was blowing hard, swirling in gusts, peppering my face with little icy pellets. Each time it blew like that, it found cracks in my clothes, letting in snow that lay icy against my neck and wrists, and it made me glad again that I hadn't woken Leila. Neither of us had had new coats or boots in a while, and without proper warm clothes, she'd be better off warm in bed.

I looked toward Sarah's house, big and square and sturdy-looking there on the sloping hill, the barns and outhouses also big and solid. I could see light in the kitchen of their house, and I pictured Sarah's mother helping Sarah into her warm coat, bundling her up against the cold.

Sarah's family are Quakers — plain people, they're sometimes called — and they're different in some ways from other people. Sarah's clothes are plain, with no bows or lace or bold colors like some of the other girls wear. Her father and uncles and brothers wear big, wide-brimmed hats, and the older ones all have beards. The older people also say "thee" and "thou," instead of "you," although Sarah and her brothers don't talk like that. But the most important thing about them is that they seem to think differently from other people — at least that's what Mama says. Mama says they don't care at all about the world, about important things like money, and I think that maybe that's true. But she also says Quakers don't care about ownership, that they'll even take things that are properly owned by others — and that I don't believe at all.

When Mama talks like that, her face twists up, and I know she's talking about slaves. Mama grew up in New Orleans, and she believes that people are allowed to own other people — own Negroes. She's says it's natural law. I don't say anything about that, even though I think she's wrong. I just let her say it, and I try to forgive her inside my own head. I know that money, and our lack of it lately, makes her have mean thoughts sometimes, maybe because we once had so much.

Mama often reminds me that I'm allowed to have Quaker friends like Sarah, as long as I remember that I'm special, different: a sea captain's daughter, she says! What's so special about being a sea captain's daughter, Mama? I want to ask her. I don't, though. I know that she has to think we're special, maybe because that's all she has left: pride.

I shivered, backing even closer to the stable wall. It was really so very cold. Then I saw the house door open and Sarah come running down the steps and across the snow to me, and I stepped out to meet her.

She was bundled up tight, her small face just peeking above the collar of her coat, her hands in huge mittens, her books in a basket slung over her arm.

From the way she came running, I knew she had something to tell me — gossip. A secret. When she got closer, I saw I was right, saw her eyes were bright.

"What?" I said before she could even speak.

"Secrets!" she said, grabbing my hand. Hers were warm, mittened, and she held mine tight. "Where's Leila?"

"She isn't well," I said. "What secrets?"

"Listen!" she said, tugging me down the alley to the street. "First, did you hear about Mr. Hathaway? Our teacher?"

"What about him?" I said.

Sarah turned to me, smiling, showing her dimples, her white, even teeth with the tiny gap between the two front ones. She hates that gap, says it makes her ugly, but I think it makes her smile especially sweet.

"The school board is going to call on him to answer for his beliefs about slavery!" she said. "Papa and Brother Foster and Edgar's papa were talking about it at our house last night." Her eyes sparkled even more, and she squeezed my hand hard. "Edgar was there with his papa. Want to know what Edgar said about you?"

I shrugged. "If you care to tell," I said.

"If I care to tell!" she said, laughing, mimicking me. "Yes, I care to tell. He says you're the smartest one in the whole class. Admit it! Admit you like Edgar! I know you do."

"I certainly do not!" I said.

Sarah giggled. "Quakers don't lie," she said.

"I'm not a Quaker!" I said back. "But I don't lie, either."

I pulled away from her, pulling my hands farther up inside my sleeves. I glared at her, but suddenly I couldn't help smiling. She was probably right — a little bit, anyway. It's so confusing. Sometimes I find myself looking across the classroom at Edgar, hoping he'll look back at me. And then if he does, I want to hide, disappear, like a mouse.

We turned the corner onto Market Street then, turned directly into the wind that blew the snow like tiny knives into our faces.

"Look, Genevieve!" Sarah said, her voice a whisper. "There he is. Edgar! Edgar and that stupid Joke Daniels."

I quick took her hand again, moving closer to her.

Edgar and Joke were there by the corner, looking at a signboard outside the butcher shop. Someone had posted a reward sign there — a reward for runaway slaves. I'd passed it many times this past week. It's been torn down a few times, but always a new one appears in its place.

As we approached, part of me wanted to stop and say hello to Edgar. Part of me didn't. The part that didn't won, so Sarah and I walked on past, pretending not to notice either of them. Yet we couldn't help overhearing what they were saying. Or what Joke was saying. He was talking loud, as though he wanted everyone in the village to hear.

"A hundred dollars!" he said, pointing a fat finger at the poster. "I could earn a hundred dollars. And if I couldn't find me a runaway, I could find me a free one and turn him in instead."

"You wouldn't turn anyone in!" Edgar answered.

"Would, too," Joke said. "It's legal, too. The Fugitive Slave Law makes it legal — just ask Mr. Hathaway. You heard him. There's no higher law than the law of the land — he said so himself."

"Except for God's law," Edgar said.

Sarah clutched my arm even tighter. "Oh, I do like Edgar!" she whispered. "Too bad he's sweet on *you*."

"He is not sweet on me!" I said. "And Joke is a pig!"

"A fat one!" she said.

We walked on, but when we were past, I couldn't help turning to take a quick look over my shoulder,

15

thinking of what Sarah had just told me — that Edgar thought I was the smartest one in the class! To my shame, he was watching me, watching me turn to look at him.

I quick turned back again. "Why is the school board calling on Mr. Hathaway?" I asked, more to change the subject than because I cared very much.

"For the same thing that Joke was talking about," she said. "His support for the Fugitive Slave Law. Remember what he said in class? Isn't it scary?"

I nodded. It was scary, strange and scary, the whole thing. Lately there had been much talk about runaway slaves, not only from Mr. Hathaway and from Mama, but also in town and in the churches, ever since the Fugitive Slave Law had been passed, and especially now that the bounty hunters and the federal marshal had come to town. The law, the United States law, said that you had to return a runaway slave if one was found and that if you hid a slave, you were breaking the law. Yet slavery was against our law, Massachusetts law! A lot of people here in New Bedford hated that Fugitive Slave Law. But it was whispered that at least a few people were likely to turn in a slave if one was found. Not only that, but free Negroes were sometimes captured in the North and sold into slavery in the South, just as Joke said he'd do — although I didn't really believe he would. He just blusters and jokes. It's how he got his name. Yet even nice people lately had been doing awful things, like what they'd done with Anthony Burns, the escaped slave captured in Boston, the riots and killing, then finally marching him off in chains to a slave ship. It was scary, all the evil feelings about.

"Sarah?" I said. "Do you think slavery's a sin?"

"Papa says it is," she said.

"Do you?" I asked.

Sarah shrugged. "I don't know. Do you?"

I made a face. "I'm not sure what sin is," I said. I couldn't help admitting to myself, though, that, sin or not, I understood why Joke could at least think of doing what he said he'd do. One hundred dollars!

Sarah sighed. "It's worrisome, slavery is," she said. "But it's also boring. That's all that Papa and Brother Foster and Edgar's papa talked about last night. Why are Quakers so dull!"

I laughed. "You're a Quaker," I said. "You're not dull."

"Do you think I will be someday?" Sarah said very seriously. "Boring and dull, I mean? When I get old?"

I smiled. "No," I said. "Anyway, I don't think we're ever going to get old, you and me. Not old the way other people get old."

A horse and buggy splashed past us then, sending wet snow sloshing toward us and over our feet. We backed away fast, and I tried to pull my neck deeper inside my coat collar. The snow was really coming down thick and hard.

"Slavery doesn't matter, anyway, right?" Sarah said. "There aren't any slaves here. Besides, there's another secret. You didn't ask what it was." She made a pretend mad face at me.

"What is it?" I asked.

She lowered her voice again. "You know about the headlamps and how they send on messages about ships coming in and cargoes and all?"

I nodded. Everybody knew about that. There were messages sent by lamps or beacons, flashing messages that told what ships were coming and what cargoes they were bringing. It was done in code, but if you understood the code, as most sailors did, the messages were easy to read.

"Yes?" I said.

"Well," Sarah said, and she shuddered, not like she was really frightened, but more like she was having fun scaring herself. "At supper when Brother Foster was talking, he said a ghost ship was coming."

"Ghost ship?" I said. "What's that?"

Again she shuddered. "I don't know for sure," she said. "I asked Brother Foster, but Papa said, 'Little pitchers have big ears,' and he sent me away to help Mama clear the table. So all I know is what Brother

Foster said: ghost ship. Know what I think it is? I think it's probably a ship that just drifts, where the crew is all dead, don't you? All filled with ghosts!"

Suddenly I could feel my heart begin to beat wildly in my throat. Leila had been listening for a ship the night before, that night and all those other nights. What if the ship she was listening for turned out to be a ghost ship?

"Do you think it's true?" I asked, and my voice came out almost in a whisper.

"I don't know," Sarah answered. "Probably not. But it's fun to imagine, isn't it?"

I folded my arms tightly across my stomach.

Could it be true? But Leila would have known that, wouldn't she?

Or would she?

Suddenly Sarah turned to me, her eyes wide. "Oh, Gen!" she burst out. "I'm sorry. It's not — I mean, I know that your papa's ship has gone down — I mean, is lost — I mean, hasn't been heard from. But it can't be his ship. That was so stupid of me."

"It doesn't matter," I answered.

It did matter, though. It mattered so much. Because it was all right to hope and pray for Papa to come home. It was even all right to give up hope as I'd done finally, sure that his ship had gone down after three years and not a word. It wasn't all right, though, to picture him on a ghost ship, dead with all his companions, corpses drifting on the seas.

But no! I didn't believe in a ghost ship.

I did not believe in a ghost ship at all.

⤳ Chapter Three ⤶

By the time school was over that day, the snow was
blinding, swept in on a howling north wind. Mr. Hathaway sent us home in groups, assigned to look out for
one another.

I was paired with Sarah because she lived next door,
and Edgar and Joke Daniels were told to see us home.
Edgar!

I didn't dare look at Sarah as we got into our coats
and boots and collected our lunch pails, but I knew,
even without looking, that she was smiling at me. I
also knew my face was flaming hot.

Once outside in the snow, I clutched Sarah's arm
tightly, fighting against the wind that seemed to want
to tear our breath away. But it was hard to walk without slipping, and I kept feeling my feet sliding sideways, even as Sarah and I held on to each other

fiercely. And then, I thought I would die when Edgar suddenly came up alongside and took hold of my free arm. Took my arm and held it as tightly as Sarah held the other one.

I pretended not to notice, didn't say a word, but the place where he touched me felt hot as the farrier's hot iron.

Joke Daniels came up on Sarah's other side but made no move to help or steady her, and I wondered if I should shake off Edgar's hand.

I didn't.

We turned the corner from school, none of us speaking, with the wind tearing at us like that, then came into sight of the docks, barely visible off to our left, where the tall sailing ships were tied up. I remembered what Sarah had said that morning about the ghost ship, and suddenly I shuddered. Shuddered and slipped, my feet going out from under me. I landed in the snow, right on my seat, my skirts spread out around me, my petticoat and even my knees showing.

"Gen!" Sarah cried.

I was struggling to get my skirts down over my knees as Edgar reached for my hands, grabbing them and hauling me to my feet, so he and I were really close, face to face.

"Genevieve!" he said. "Are you all right?"

"I'm fine!" I said, but it came out all angry and rude because I felt so foolish. "You can let go now," I said.

He let go of my hands, and I brushed the snow from my clothes, and he took my arm again.

"You looked just like Daisy!" Joke said, laughing.

"Daisy?" I said.

"Our sow," Joke said. "When she falls in her slops."

"You're disgusting," Sarah said.

Joke just shrugged.

We turned then onto the hill that led up to our houses, turned and found ourselves facing directly into the wind. I bent my head, squinting against the snow.

"I can't see a thing," Sarah gasped. "What if we get lost?"

"We won't," Edgar said. "You live up the hill. The wind is coming from the hill. We just keep facing into the wind."

"What if the wind changes direction?" Joke said.

"It's a northerly wind," Edgar said quietly. "They don't blow out that fast."

"My pa says there's a devil's wind," Joke said. "It changes direction and goes round and round and . . ."

He was whirling his arms round and round, as if to show us a devil's wind, when suddenly he stopped and stared. "Hey!" he said. "What's that?"

He pointed to a stone wall, off to our right, barely visible through the swirling snow.

Someone, a person, was huddled there. At least it looked like a person.

A person out here! Whoever it was would surely freeze to death — if they hadn't already.

"Wait here a minute!" Edgar said, letting go of my arm.

He made his way over to the wall, lifting his feet high over drifts, Joke lumbering after him.

Sarah and I followed, then watched as they bent over the figure.

"Who is it?" I asked, trying to see over their bent backs.

"Just old Joe," Joke said, straightening up and pushing his hands down into his pockets, his shoulders hunched against the wind. "Simon Joe."

"Simon Joe!" I said. "Is he all right?"

"Don't think so," Joke said. "Probably dead."

"No!" I said.

Simon Joe was one of the few Negroes in town. He worked on the docks as a watchman and lived in a small shack back behind this field. He has fits sometimes where he falls down in a swoon or a faint — some people say it's caused by the devil — but Sarah's papa says it's just an illness, that it can happen to anybody. Everybody knows about it, and most people help him when he's found lying somewhere.

"He's not dead, Joke!" Edgar said, raising his voice

to be heard over the wind. "We have to get him warm, though, or he will be."

He began pulling at Joe, trying to tug him up to his feet. "Come on!" he said. "Come on, Joe! Get up."

Joke made a face. "He's probably drunk. Let him be. Let's go."

"Leave him here?" I said.

"Why not?" Joke said.

"Because he'll freeze to death!" Sarah said.

Joke just shrugged. "He won't. He'll come to."

"Come on, Joke!" Edgar said, looking over his shoulder at Joke, squinting against the swirling snow. "At least help me get him on his feet."

Joke folded his arms across his chest. "I ain't touching him," he said.

I handed Sarah my lunch pail. "Hold this!" I said.

I tried to push Joke aside then, but it was like pushing at a stone wall. When he didn't move, I stepped around his huge bulk, then bent over Joe, who was half crouched, half lying in the snow. One eye was open, following my every move, but the other was swollen shut, a thick streak of dried blood high on his cheekbone.

"He looks like he hit the wall when he fell," Edgar said to me. "Maybe had a fit?"

I shrugged. I didn't know what had happened, but I knew we had to get him up.

"Joe?" I said. "Can you get up?"

He groaned.

I took one of his arms, and Edgar took the other.

"We won't hurt you," I said. "Can you help us help you?"

Again he groaned, but this time he nodded slightly.

It took some doing, tugging and pulling at him and losing our own footing, but finally he got his feet under him and we were able to pull him upright.

"Lord!" he whispered once he was standing. He pulled himself free of our hands. "Lord, Lord!" he said again.

He stood looking down at himself, at his clothes stiff with ice and snow. He blinked a few times, took a faltering step, and then stopped.

"Are you all right?" Edgar said.

Joe blinked again, letting his eyes stay closed for a long minute, swaying a little where he stood. He put a hand on the bloodied place on his face.

"Joe?" Edgar said. "Can you get home from here?" Where do you live?"

Joe opened his eyes. "Just over there," he said, his voice soft and hoarse. He lifted his arm just the tiniest bit, as though trying to point to the field. "There. I'll make it just fine."

I looked where he was trying to point, but through the snow, his house wasn't visible, although I knew it was at the back of that field.

"Now can we go?" Joke said. "Before we all freeze to death?"

Edgar looked at Joke and Sarah and me, then back at Joe. "Are you sure you can make it all right?" he asked.

"I can," Joe said quietly. "God bless."

He turned away then, and we watched as he slowly climbed over the wall. He took a few steps into the field, staggering a bit, his footprints making a wobbly line in the snow. Then, practically within seconds, he disappeared from our sight into the swirling maze of snow.

I heard Edgar sigh, saw him staring at the place where Joe had disappeared, and I wondered if he was thinking what I was thinking: Perhaps we should have seen Joe home?

I shoved my hands deeper into my pockets as Sarah moved closer to me, tucking her arm through mine again. Her teeth were actually chattering, and she looked just about frozen, her nose dripping, the snow piling up on her coat collar that she had pulled up around her face. She huddled against me, but she was staring off into the field, too. I also noticed Joke looking in that direction, a worried, anxious look on his face, and I couldn't help remembering what he'd said that morning.

As if he knew what I was thinking, he spoke, very softly. "I was just funning this morning," he said, his voice kind of muffled, embarrassed-sounding. "I wouldn't turn in nobody. Especially not a free one."

None of us answered, although Edgar nodded.

I shuddered. There was so much that was ugly and confusing. But thinking about Simon Joe, there was one thing that wasn't confusing, one thing I knew for sure: Simon Joe wasn't safe. Even if Joke had just been funning, Simon Joe just plain wasn't safe.

The four of us stood there for just a moment more, then turned again into the wind, heading home.

⌒ Chapter Four ⌒

When I finally got home that day, I found Leila seated in her little rocking chair by the fire in the back parlor, drawing yet another bird in her little sketchbook. Actually it's not much of a sketchbook, more a collection of some partially used writing paper and pieces of butcher paper that I'd trimmed and bound for her with a bit of string. She was carefully drawing an enormous bird, a falcon, copying it line by line from that huge bird book that Papa brought home from one of his voyages. As I looked over her shoulder, she turned the book away from me, the way she often does. She's really a very good artist, but shy about her work.

She closed the book then and smiled up at me, a sweet smile, yet she seemed worried, a small crease between her eyes. She sent a look across the room, to where Mama sat in her usual place at the window, staring off toward the harbor, hidden by the swirls of snow.

I nodded at Leila, then crossed the room to Mama, bent, and kissed her cheek.

"I'm home, Mama," I said. I spoke softly, very softly, so as not to startle her, because sometimes even a voice could startle Mama. Besides, I knew Leila's look was warning me that Mama was particularly fragile that day.

Mama didn't look at me, just reached up and felt for my hand, then found it and held it. "Is it terrible out, then?" she asked.

"Yes, it's terrible, Mama," I answered. "We could hardly see a foot ahead of us, but the boys walked Sarah and me home."

I didn't add anything about Simon Joe, didn't want to get her all agitated. But I did wonder if Simon Joe had been as lucky as Sarah and me in making it home.

"Ah, yes!" Mama said. "God provides. I lose faith sometimes till I remind myself: God will provide."

"How do you feel today, Mama?" I asked, still quietly.

She turned away from the window. "I'm well," she said, looking up at me. "And I have a surprise for you."

There was a strange light in her eyes, a happy look, one I rarely saw there anymore.

"What is it, Mama?" I asked, feeling my own mood rise with hers.

She got to her feet, and behind me, I could hear Leila put down her book and get to her feet, too, the rocking chair thumping emptily as she stood.

"Come," Mama said, taking my hand. "I'll show you."

She led me out of the parlor and down the drafty hall toward the kitchen, Leila following. The hall was cold, and I knew the kitchen would be, too, until later when I lit the fire for supper. I thought of Simon Joe again, hoped he had made it home, wondered if his house was colder even than ours.

To my surprise, Mama didn't go on to the kitchen, but stopped instead at the door to the dining room, a room we hadn't used in over a year.

There, she threw open the door, then stepped back, giving me a little push ahead of her into the room.

The first thing I noticed was the warmth. This room was usually bitter cold, the way rooms get when closed up, without a fire or human beings to bring them to life. Now, though, the room was almost too warm, with a fire blazing in the hearth, one that had certainly been going for hours.

In the center of the room was the table, covered now with Mama's special white damask cloth. The table was set for a meal, with the china and silver and glassware that Mama used when Papa was home, when she and Papa had their grand parties. There was no food on any of the plates, but there were many dishes at each place — soup plates and salad plates and dinner plates and bread-and-butter plates, and at each place, three different kinds of glasses for three different kinds of wine. In the center of the table was a mirrored centerpiece, skiers and skating ladies surrounding a mirrored lake, another of the treasures Papa had once brought home.

Across the room on the sideboard, more dishes were set out — all empty: a soup tureen with its ladle resting on a silver saucer beside it, a huge meat platter, a vegetable dish on its warmer, those thin china cups you can almost see through and their fragile saucers, a sugar bowl and creamer.

A party. The room was set for a dinner party. Just like old times.

I looked at the table again. In spite of the many kinds of dishes for many different courses, however, I saw that everything was arranged into just three place settings: three. Mama's. Leila's. Mine. Then why all the fancy fuss? Why the waste of our precious firewood and the few remaining pieces of coal?

I turned to the doorway, where Mama still stood, one hand clutching her shawl tightly around her shoulders, the other picking feverishly at her skirt. The expression on her face was feverish, too, as though she were asking me for something.

Next to Mama, Leila stood, twisting her hands round and round under her pinafore, a pinafore I hadn't really noticed before. The pinafore meant she had been working with Mama — probably setting up this room, cleaning the china and silver, carrying in the firewood.

But why? Whatever had possessed Mama?

As if in answer to my silent question, Mama said, "Why not?"

"Why not what, Mama?" I asked carefully.

Mama's eyes roamed over the table and the sideboard, deliberately avoiding mine, I thought. "Why not have a feast?" she said. "A rejoicing? It's been far too long since we used our best things. Far too long."

She let her eyes meet mine then, and that anxious, almost pleading look was still there. "When your papa comes home," she said, her voice quavering, "it will drive him to distraction to see how we've been living, don't you see? Taking meals in the kitchen as though we were no more than Quakers! I'm a sea captain's wife! You girls are sea captain's daughters. Don't you see that?"

I took a deep breath. "Yes, Mama," I said quietly. "I can see that."

Mama threw her arms wide. "I'm glad, then!" she

said. "We're going to enjoy! Dinner tonight will be in style!"

I stole a look at Leila. Seldom have I seen her look so forlorn, her little face screwed up tight, frowning hard in that way she has that I know means she is fighting back tears.

I thought I knew why, too, thought I knew what she was thinking, the same thing I was thinking: And what will we put on those plates, Mama? Cornmeal mush, the only thing left in the house? Or shall we go and beg more credit at the store?

It wouldn't help at all to say that, though, the same as it wouldn't help to argue about sea captains' daughters or Quakers' daughters. So all I said was, "Know something, Mama? I think you should go back to the parlor. Leila and I will make a grand supper tonight."

I crossed the room and took her hands. "Please go sit, Mama. Will you do that for me?"

She nodded. "You'll summon me to dinner?"

"Summon you?" I said, forcing a cheerful voice. "I'll come and escort you!" I took her hand, tucking it through my arm. "Like this!" I said.

"Oh, you are your father's daughter," Mama said, and she gently removed my hand and started for the door. But at the doorway, she stopped and turned. "We'll have a feast tonight?" she asked. "Promise?"

"I promise, Mama," I said.

I waited till she had closed the door, then turned to Leila. "What happened?" I said. "Do you know? Why this, today?"

"Oh, Gen!" she said, tucking her hands under her pinafore and twisting them round and round again. "I think it's my fault. See, I was listening this morning, on the stairs, because I felt as sure as I felt last night that I'd hear a ship. Mama saw me and decided it was his ship, Papa's ship, I was listening for."

"Isn't it?" I said impatiently. "Isn't that what you've been listening for? Why? When you know it can't be Papa's. You know it! No ship goes unheard from for three years!"

Unless . . .

"Leila?" I said. I swallowed hard. "Leila, what if he's dead? What if he's dead, him and his whole crew, if they're all dead, floating on the seas? Could it be a ghost ship that's coming?"

She frowned at me. "Dead?" she said. "Ghosts? He's not dead."

I just shook my head. I wanted so much to believe her, to believe in her powers, her knowledge.

If only I could believe.

I sighed. "All right," I said. "Let's go now and try and find some food to put on these plates."

"Gen," Leila said quietly when we were back in the

kitchen. "There's something else. Mama sent me to Mr. Archer's store today."

"In this weather?" I said. "When I didn't wake you up just so you wouldn't have to go out!"

Leila just shrugged. "It wasn't that bad," she said. "But listen. Mr. Archer, he wouldn't give me everything on Mama's list, I think because Mama wanted so much, even a whole ham! Mr. Archer gave me only some cornmeal and salt pork and bread, and he says Mama has to come and talk to him about settling up the bill before he'll give us more."

I sighed. I'd heard things like this before from Mr. Archer. He'd been grumbling a lot about credit lately. It was embarrassing, but he always gave us the food, although Leila and I tried to ask for only the most basic things we needed. "He'll be all right," I said. "He'll forget he said that next time."

Leila shook her head. "I don't think so," she said. "I think he meant it. From now on, no more credit."

I looked sharply at her. "Those were his very words?" I asked.

She nodded. "Yes, and he said he meant it. He said he needed some commitment from Mama."

I rubbed my hands over my face and shook my head, then looked again at Leila. "Did you tell Mama?" I asked.

Leila nodded.

"What did she say?" I asked.

Leila looked down at her foot, then up at me. " 'God will provide,' " she whispered.

She said it in this tiny, faint voice that sounded so much like Mama's that I just burst out laughing.

Leila looked surprised for a moment; then she began laughing, too.

"How did you learn that?" I said. "It was perfect."

Leila giggled. "I've been practicing," she said.

I laughed again and shook my head. Leila is a wonderful mimic and always has been. It's especially funny the way she mimics people at school.

But I was awfully worried. We were cold and didn't have proper clothes, and Mama was ill — at least her mind wasn't right — and the house was in need of repairs. I could hear a loose shutter that very minute, banging in the wind. And now we'd be hungry — well, we'd been hungry for a while, but now we'd be even more hungry than before.

I took a deep breath.

Something. It was time to do something. And there was no one to do it but me.

⇜ Chapter Five ⇝

Next morning I slid quietly out of bed, long before the sun was up. There would probably be no school, because it was still snowing wildly, but I had to go out anyway. I had a plan, something I had to do.

Dinner had been so awful the night before — the table set so brilliantly but with only cornmeal mush and a little salt pork and bread — and Mama trying so desperately to be bright and funny, then lapsing into silence.

After I had gone to bed, I'd lain awake for a long time, thinking. Maybe, I'd thought, Mama was right and one day God would provide. And maybe, too, Leila was right — although I didn't really believe it — and Papa would one day come home.

But meanwhile, who could keep us from starving?

There was only one person. And that person was me.

I lay there working out many different plans, but none of them seemed quite right — working as a housemaid or nursemaid for one of the other sea captains in town, because they had money and many live-in maids, or getting on the stagecoach when it came through and going to work in one of the mills in New Salem. People said girls were getting paid two dollars a week for working in the mills! Talking to one of the Quaker families and asking for work on their farm. I even had the bizarre thought that I could disguise myself as a boy and get hired on one of the ships. Heavens knew my body was still flat as a boy's.

But how could I do any of those things when Mama continued to pretend, as she'd done the day before, that all was well? Unless I dared to go against her, behind her back? Some days she barely noticed anything. . . .

It was very late when I thought of a plan that might work. I had fallen asleep and had been dreaming and then awoke, knowing exactly what it was I had to do.

Now in the morning, I dressed silently, without building up the fire in our room so as not to wake Leila, then tiptoed downstairs to the kitchen.

There, I fixed the fire in the stove and set about getting ready to go out into the storm.

First I put on my own coat and on top of it, an old oilskin of Papa's. It had hung for more than three years on a peg inside the back door, waiting there like an old, friendly ghost. When I put it on, it felt stiff and cold; still, I knew it would cut the wind and protect me from the wet.

Next I found some boots of Mama's, since mine no longer fit, and pulled them on. Mama wouldn't care. She hadn't been out of the house in almost a year, anyway. Then I wrapped a huge old scarf around my neck and pulled on an old woolen stocking cap.

When I was all dressed, I looked down at myself. I looked all lumpy and misshapen, but I'd be warm enough, at least warmer than yesterday, and if my plan worked, someday soon there'd be a little money. We could buy some clothes then, at least the important things like boots for Leila and me.

I started for the back door and saw, on the table there, the list Mama had sent to the store with Leila yesterday.

I picked it up and read it. The first thing on it was a ham — *a whole ham,* she had written, underlining the world *whole.*

No wonder Mr. Archer had become angry with her!

I stuck the list in my pocket, then opened the back door and stepped down — sinking into snow that came right up to my waist.

Some good these boots were! They were already filled with snow!

I made my way around to the front of the house, the snow so deep I had to use my arms to help me, the way a swimmer does, pushing through the surf. I kept my head bent against the wind, sometimes shielding my face with one arm when the wind blew particularly hard, sending the sleet and snow like tiny needles against my cheeks.

Once around the front of the house, I walked in the middle of the street, at least what I thought was the street, because it was smoother-looking there, with no big drifts of snow that might hide stone walls or something to trip over.

There were no horses or carriages out yet — carriage wheels couldn't possibly pass through these drifts — and I didn't see anyone on foot, either.

And then I had a worrisome thought: What if there was no one at Mr. Archer's store? What if the store was closed?

No. Mr. Archer lived right behind the store, no more than a little alley to cross between his place and the store. He'd be there. Besides, he didn't own the store, only ran it for Brother Foster. If Mr. Archer wasn't there, surely the owner would be?

I kept my head bent and plowed forward, finally reaching the corner, then turning down the hill toward town. It was easier going on the downhill, maybe because the wind had swept away some of the snow.

Ahead, I could see the store and could see that at least one horse stood tethered there.

So there was someone there!

I half slipped, half slid my way down the hill. In front of the store, a narrow path had been shoveled, but it was already filling in again with new snow. I hurried across the path, opened the door, and stepped in.

A fire was burning in the iron stove in the middle of the room, and even from all the way over by the door, I could feel the heat. I crossed the room and stood in front of it, my hands outstretched to the warmth. Someone had obviously been here for a long while, for the fire to be so hot. But although I heard voices in back, no one was about.

I was just wondering whether to call out and announce myself when Mr. Archer appeared from the back room. As soon as he saw me, he came directly over to the stove, frowning — frowning because I had the nerve to come here begging again after what he had said to Leila just yesterday?

"Yes?" he said. "May I help you?"

When he was closer, though, he suddenly smiled. "Why it's Genevieve!" he said. "Miss Genevieve. In such a getup! What brings you out on a morning like this?"

"It's not what you think!" I blurted out, and then

could have bitten off my tongue for saying that. "I mean," I said, "what I mean is, would you —"

I stopped. I looked down at my feet, watched the snow slowly melt and drip off my boots. Now that the moment was actually here, it seemed so ridiculous. How could I make such an unheard-of proposition? Girls don't work in stores! Girls don't work at all. Even women hardly ever have jobs, except as schoolteachers maybe or like Miss Mattie, who works in the milliner's shop.

But most girls' papas are not lost at sea.

"Something wrong?" Mr. Archer said at last. "Someone ill at home?"

I looked up. He has large, furry eyebrows, like commas over his eyes, and they were pulled together in a deep frown. But his look was kind, worried almost.

"No," I said. "No one is ill."

"Good," he said, and he waited.

"Work!" I blurted out. "I wondered if you needed someone to work for you." The words suddenly tumbled over each other in the rush to get out. "I remember hearing you say last summer how you needed someone to deliver packages and sweep up, so do you still need that someone?"

Mr. Archer nodded. "I surely do," he said. "If you find someone, send him to me. We'll talk. However, I'm not sure you can find the person I need. I don't believe there's a boy in this town who works hard enough to satisfy me."

That's where he was wrong, though. There was a person who would work that hard. But could I find the courage to tell him that the boy — the person — was me?

Mr. Archer turned and walked away from me then, over to the counter, where he opened up the cash drawer. He began taking out bills and coins and laying them on the countertop, organizing them into separate piles. "Although," he said, not looking up from his coins, "I guess that isn't what brought you out on a morning like this, is it?"

"But it is!" I said. And then I did it, said the very words I'd been trying so hard to say. "I'd like to be the boy — I mean the person — who works for you."

At that, Mr. Archer did look up. "You?" he said, putting his hands on the counter and leaning forward to peer at me.

"Yes," I said, feeling my heart pound wildly in my throat, feeling the heat creep up my cheeks.

He frowned. "You're a girl," he said.

"Yes," I said.

"And a young one at that!" he added.

I nodded. To myself I said, Not that young!

"You go to school, don't you?" he asked, pulling his furry eyebrows even closer together.

"Yes," I said.

He turned back to the cash drawer, put the money in, and slammed the drawer shut. Then he came out from behind the counter and crossed the room to where I stood by the stove. "I can't do that, Miss Genevieve," he said quietly. "I can't let you work."

"Why not?" I said, looking straight at him and trying to make myself look older, taller, or something. "I'm really a good worker. I'd work very hard!"

"I'm sure of that," he answered, smiling slightly. He held out his hand. "Where's your mama's list?" he said quietly. "I'll fill her order. I'm afraid I wasn't very kind to Miss Leila yesterday."

I looked down at my feet, fighting back the tears, the feeling of helplessness. Didn't he know how much I needed this job?

"Come!" Mr. Archer said, his hand still outstretched, and I could see it even though my head was bent. "Give me the list. It's all right."

I shook my head.

"What is it thee wants?" a voice said from behind me.

I spun around.

Brother Foster was standing close behind me, his face huge, red, and chapped-looking from wind and sun. He has a full, reddish beard and reddish side-whiskers, and for one ridiculous moment, I thought of Saint Nicholas.

"What is it thee wants?" he repeated.

"Work?" I said, and even though I intended to sound grown up and strong, my voice came out just a little above a whisper.

"Food," Mr. Archer said behind me, speaking quietly over my head. "This is the family we spoke of, the friend of Sarah's? I should have realized how bad things were for them, although I must say I knew things weren't well. Their papa's been gone a good long while —"

"Not food!" I said, and I could feel tears swim into my eyes, making me so furious. I didn't want to cry. "Work!" I said, and it came out all fierce.

"Art thou a good worker?" Brother Foster asked, bending to look into my eyes, his face close to mine.

I took a deep breath and looked back at him. "Yes," I said. "I mean, I work hard." It was the most honest answer I could give.

"We'll give the family more credit," Mr. Archer said behind me. "They need food, and her sister —"

"Nay," Brother Foster interrupted, holding up a huge, rough-looking hand. "I think the lass needs work. If she's from the family we spoke of, I think thou should give her a chance."

A chance! I clapped, then remembered it was time

to be grown up. I put my hands by my side and stood up straighter.

I turned back to Mr. Archer then, but I was so nervous that when I spoke, my voice actually trembled. "I'll work really hard," I said. "You won't be sorry — I promise."

He didn't answer. Instead he again looked over my head at Brother Foster, his eyebrows raised. "Do we need another set of eyes around here?" he asked quietly.

Brother Foster tilted his head to one side and looked closely at me again, a calm, careful look. "I believe this is a lass we can trust," he said at last.

Trust? Because of the money in the store? Or something to do with eyes, whatever that meant?

"When can thou begin work?" Brother Foster asked me.

"Now!" I said. "Right this very minute."

He laughed and shook his head. "Not in this storm. Go on home, and come back tomorrow. If the storm has stopped, we'll look for thee tomorrow. Now, give us thy mother's list."

But I couldn't do that. There was enough food at home from what Mr. Archer had given Leila yesterday, enough for a few days at least. "It's all right," I said quietly. "We have enough."

Brother Foster laughed, a big booming sound.

"Don't be shy!" he said. "Thou shall be working for it. Soon we may even owe thee!" And he held out his hand for the list.

I couldn't help looking up then and laughing with him. Him? Owe me?

The very thought!

≈ Chapter Six ≈

No more begging. No more being hungry. No more credit. And something to count on. You can't simply go day to day with no future, planning nothing, begging money as you go along, trusting God to feed you — God and the neighborhood merchant. Nobody ever told Mama that, but I knew it. And as I sat in the parlor with Mama and Leila that afternoon, waiting out the storm, only one thing about my plan made me sad: school. I'd miss school, because in spite of my complaining sometimes, I really do like my studies, arithmetic and reading especially. I'd miss Sarah, too, her more than anything.

And then a little voice inside me said, And Edgar? Hush! I told it.

I smiled then, thinking of Papa, how he always talked back to his voice from within — his conscience, he called it — sometimes even answering it out loud. I didn't know if my inner voice was a conscience or not, but it was certainly a nuisance, one that continually argued with me.

Thinking of Papa, I reached in my pocket and felt for my pocket watch. It isn't one of those tiny lady's timepieces that you can hardly read. This is a big one that Papa gave me one Christmas, one just like his, with a big fat face and big hands and loud ticking. I don't carry it with me all the time, because I'm afraid of losing it. Mostly it stays on my bedside table. I could hear it there, as I drifted off to sleep, counting out the minutes, the hours, the days, and months — and years — that Papa'd been gone. Sometimes, though, like on that day, I carried it, just for comfort, just to remind me of Papa. I missed him so much. When he was home, he'd called me his little sea captain, took me everywhere he went around town, even down to the docks. The sailors would laugh and ask Papa if he thought I'd grow up to be a sailor girl. Papa would smile at me and say, "She can be anything she wants to be." He really believed in me, believed I could do anything I wanted to do. What would he think of me now? I wondered. Would he be proud of me for going to Mr. Archer? Or would he think the way Mama did — that I should have pride in being a sea captain's daughter, enough pride to wait for God to provide?

I sighed then and looked around the room. For hours, I had been thinking out these things while I did my needlepoint, sitting next to Leila, who was sketching, across the room from Mama, who kept vigil by the window. The snow was still falling, the storm howling and raging and beating itself against the town as though it would never tire and go away. I got up and went to stand beside Mama, looking out at the storm. It had been two whole days that it had been snowing, and deep drifts covered everything: the docks, the ships at harbor, the fields and barns and houses. I could barely see to the harbor, could see only the shadowlike outlines of ships, their tops hidden in the swirling snow, could hear the creaking and sighing of the masts as they groaned and protested the wind. And that wind! It howled and bit and assaulted everything in its path, shaking the windows and seeming to send shivering drafts of cold air right through the windowpanes and into the room.

I looked down at Mama. She had been extra quiet since our "dinner party" the other night, maybe thinking how hard it had become to keep up the pretense — or maybe thinking something else entirely, because it was hard to tell with Mama. She was looking out, but there was a strange blank kind of look on her face, as though only her body were there but she were not.

"Mama?" I said softly.

She didn't answer.

"Mama?" I said again, bending close and putting a hand gently on her hair. "Are your eyes tired? Would you like me to read to you?"

She looked up, blinking. "Yes?" she said.

"I asked if you want me to read to you. If your eyes are tired, I could read aloud. It would make the time pass. Would you like to hear some Scriptures, the Psalms, maybe?"

Mama sighed, her breath shaky. "I have a headache," she said.

"Shall I get you something?" I asked. "A tonic, a tisane?"

I knew we still had herbs in the house, and I could make something up for her.

Mama shook her head. "No, no," she whispered. "It wouldn't help." She closed her eyes and rested her head back against the chair. Her hair is thick and dark, with hardly any gray in it, and it fell now in little wisps around her face.

"Can I massage your forehead?" I asked.

Again she shook her head.

I straightened up then but stood looking down at her, feeling my heart begin to thump hard in my chest. She was so frail, so odd lately. And the headaches were more frequent than ever since winter had begun.

It was very quiet in the room, the only sound the wind whistling in the chimney and rattling the windows, making the curtains move softly outward into the room.

I looked across the room to Leila. She was watching Mama, her bottom lip pulled in between her teeth, and I had the feeling that she was holding her breath. Neither of us spoke, but I knew, and knew that Leila knew, what was about to happen. And it did.

Mama began to cry. Tears fell silently, a sudden torrent of tears, dropping from her face directly onto her hands. Her hands are thin, the blue veins clearly visible, and I could see the tiny thump of a pulse flickering there.

I reached down and took her hand, felt it limp inside my own. She just continued to cry but didn't do anything else, didn't sob, didn't take deep, shaky breaths, didn't even blow her nose. It was a deep, silent crying, seeming to come not just from her eyes but from way down inside her. Watching her, I had the odd thought that she wasn't even doing the crying, that it was just happening to her.

"It's all right, Mama," I whispered, lifting her hand to my face and kissing it. I let it go then, gently lowering it to her lap, and took out my handkerchief. Carefully I wiped her face, first one cheek, then the other, then under her chin, where the tears had run.

I was still wiping her face when suddenly there was a huge crash, somewhere outside.

Mama opened her eyes, and behind me, Leila let out a frightened little squeal.

"What is it?" Mama whispered, her eyes wide and red-rimmed.

I leaned closer to the window, peering out. It sounded like a mast breaking, a sound I remembered from a hurricane last year. I couldn't see anything, though, and I turned back to the room just as there was another crash, this one closer, louder — the sound of breaking glass, something shattering.

"A window!" Leila said. "It sounds like a window. Come, Gen!"

She jumped up from her rocker, and both of us hurried down the hall toward the front, from where the sound seemed to have come.

It wasn't hard to find what had happened. I actually felt it first, felt the cold and wind. I opened the door to the front parlor and saw a shutter that should have been repaired long ago, that had been hanging by a single rusted hinge, lying halfway through a window. It had been torn off by the wind, then hurled against the window, and it lay there, half in, half out, the window shattered.

In the few seconds it had taken Leila and me to get there from the back parlor, snow had already begun to cover the lacquered Chinese table under the window, a table Papa had brought home, one of Mama's treasures, and was piling up on the rug.

I bent and turned back the rug, shaking off the snow.

Leila was right behind me, taking the candles off the table and wiping it dry with her skirt. "It's wet, Gen!" she said. "Oh, you don't think it's ruined, do you?"

"No," I said. "No, it'll be all right."

I looked around then for something, anything, to board up the window.

Leila was looking, too.

"That!" she said, pointing to the fireplace. A decorative board, in place for summer months, stood covering the opening of the fireplace, and she hurried toward it.

I went to help her, and we dragged it across to the window, lifted it, and wedged it into place in front of the broken glass. It was close enough in size to fit somewhat tightly, although heavens knew the wind could tear it out again, and being wood, it would quickly be soaked through.

We backed up and looked at it. I could still feel the wind and the icy cold, seeping in around the edges. But it was the best we had, all we had, and at least it was keeping out the snow.

Leila and I were both quiet then, surveying the boarded-up window, the mess of broken glass. I wondered if we could leave it boarded up this way for a while, since getting repairs would certainly cost money.

"Gen?" Leila said, moving closer to me, her small face pinched and worried-looking. "What's wrong with Mama?"

"I don't know," I said. "I think she needs a doctor, though."

"Could a doctor help, you think?" Leila asked. "Could a doctor make her stop crying?"

"Yes, he could," I said, although I wasn't at all sure about that.

"Then let's send for him," she said, her voice little more than a whisper. "We have money for that, don't we?"

"Don't you worry about that," I said. "Money is for me to worry about."

"I can't help but worry," she said.

I rested a hand on her head. "Leila," I said, "can you keep a secret? From Mama? At least for a while?"

She nodded. "I can keep a secret."

I took a deep breath. "I've been worried, too," I said. "About food and money and everything. And so today I did something: I'm going to work in the store, Mr. Archer's store. I went to see him today, and he's agreed to hire me. He's going to pay me, Leila."

Leila backed away and looked at me, frowning, her head tilted to one side. "Work?" she said. "You're a girl!"

I had to laugh. She sounded so much like Mr. Archer. I moved closer to her and put a hand on her hair, giving her long braid a gentle tug. "Yes," I said. "I'm a girl. But it's honest work, Leila, and I can do it. He's already hired me. And we need the money."

She frowned down at her feet, her little face all twisted up, then looked back up at me. "But girls don't work!" she said. "Besides, even if you did, what about school? You'll miss it. And Mr. Hathaway will come round to see Mama if you're not in school."

"I'll figure that out later," I said. "And yes, I will miss it, Leila, but I need to. Besides, you know what I was thinking today? I was thinking that Papa depended on me to help the family."

She chewed on her lip. "Know what, Genevieve?" she said, reaching up and taking my hand after a minute. "I think he'll be real proud of you when he comes home. And know what else?" She smiled widely at me then, the way she does when she's just come up with a wonderful idea. "I'll bring home lessons for you — that's what I'll do. I'll tell you everything I learn in school, and I'll also listen in and learn everything that students are learning at your level. You won't miss a thing! That will help, won't it?"

"Yes," I said, smiling at her. "It will help. You can

also take care of Mama after school, read to her and talk to her. Maybe keep her from thinking about Papa. I think that's what's making her cry like that."

I pulled my hand out of Leila's then and hugged myself. The room was simply freezing, with the window smashed out like that. I looked over at it, at the glass littering the floor.

"I'll help her not to think," Leila said softly. "But Gen? Isn't it all right if she keeps on hoping, just a little tiny bit?"

I sighed and shook my head, but I couldn't help smiling. Leila is so stubborn in her beliefs when she takes it into her head to be.

"Yes," I said. "It's all right if she hopes a little." I put a hand on her hair again. "Things are going to get better, Leila. We'll have money for a doctor for Mama, and there'll be enough for food, and maybe even money for new boots, too."

Leila looked up at me, her small face suddenly wistful. "And drawing paper?" she asked quietly.

I had to laugh. "Yes," I answered. "And maybe drawing paper, too."

⁓ Chapter Seven ⁓

I slipped out of bed the next morning at seven o'clock, before Leila was awake. The snow had stopped, and although the wind still howled, I knew there would be school, and I was quite sure they'd expect me at the store. I planned to go there extra early, because I realized that I hadn't asked Mr. Archer or Brother Foster what time I should begin work. Surely it would be better to be early than late!

I built up the fire in our room so it would be warm when Leila woke up, then dressed silently and tiptoed downstairs. There, I fixed the kitchen fire, then set about getting myself something to eat. We had the ham Brother Foster had insisted I take, and I cut a thick slice and put it between two pieces of bread, even spreading the bread with butter.

I made myself some tea, adding sugar and milk liberally, then sat down to eat. Food! How wonderful food tasted, real food, something besides cornmeal mush and soft apples. Maybe, I thought, Mama was strange because she hadn't been getting proper food. At supper last night, when we had some of the ham and potatoes and pickle relish that Brother Foster had given me, Mama had looked at me across the table, actually smiling, although her eyes were still red-rimmed from her earlier weeping. "You see," she'd said softly. "God does provide. In His own time — but He does provide."

Well, maybe this hearty food would help Mama. And soon, I — not God — would be bringing home more.

As I ate breakfast, I wondered what my day would be like, what people would expect of me. I also wondered what the neighbors would say, people who saw me working in the store.

And then I had a frightening thought: What if someone saw me and then came and told Mama before I got to tell her? But no, who would tell her? Mama had no friends anymore, no one but Mrs. Morgan, who occasionally came to call — more, I thought, out of duty than friendship. Mrs. Morgan was a sea captain's wife, too, and she sometimes read Mama letters she'd received from Captain Morgan, letters sent on via cargo ships that picked up mail at various ports.

So unless she came and told, there was no one else who would.

After breakfast I dressed and set out, slipping and sliding down the hill toward the store. It was easier going than the day before, a few carriages and horses having been out already, making the street more passable, and I made it safely down the hill without a fall.

When I turned the corner to the store, I could see a light already gleaming from within. Someone was there, expecting me, although what they'd expect, I wasn't sure. We hadn't talked at all about what my duties would be.

At the store, I opened the door and found a fire was burning in the stove, warming the entire room, just as it had the other day. No one was about, although I could hear a soft murmur of voices from the back room. I crossed to the stove, where I stood for a minute, warming myself, listening to the voices in the back, to the logs snapping and shifting, to the soft sound of snow slipping along the roof.

After a while, I noticed that the voices in the back room were quiet but that outside in the alley, there were sounds, a rough voice raised in anger, then another that seemed to be trying to soothe it. Still, no one came out to greet me.

Should I call out? I wondered. Let them know I'm here? How does one act when one has a job?

Well, take off your coat — that's a start.

And where to hang it?

I looked around, feeling annoyed at myself. I was being as indecisive as Mama! Just go to the back, to that closed door that separates front from the back, where Mr. Archer came from yesterday. Go in there and tell him you're here and ask him what you're supposed to do!

I took a deep breath, then crossed to the door, turned the knob, and stepped into the dimly lit room beyond.

And choked back a scream of terror.

A man. A man appeared suddenly, slipped like a shadow from the wall. He slapped a hand across my mouth, pushing me back against the door. His hand was hard, callused, crushing my lips against my teeth.

I tried to cry out but couldn't.

He held me hard against the door, my neck and jaw aching from the force of his hand.

I could feel the blood pound in my throat as he put his other hand tightly under my chin. A knife? Was that the blade of a knife?

I hardly dared breathe or swallow.

Still holding me, he turned his face away slightly, toward the door to the back alley. He leaned toward the door as though listening.

I swallowed and tried to ease back from the pressure of his hands.

He turned back to me fiercely. "Be still!" he hissed.

Our eyes met then. His were wide and wild, black pools of fear. I wanted to look away yet couldn't. His hair was thick and curly, more curly than Papa's even, and his skin was dark. A Negro! This was — had to be — an escaped slave.

And he'd do anything to keep me quiet!

He leaned close then, so close I could feel his breath on my cheek. "I'll move my hand," he said, "if I have your word you won't cry out."

I won't.

"Promise!" he whispered at me. "You needn't swear. Give me your word. Nod."

He released the pressure of his hand just a bit, and I nodded. And nodded again, swallowing hard.

Even so, when he took his hand from my mouth, he kept it close, as though ready to clamp it back over me again.

I ran my tongue around my mouth, loosening my lips from my teeth, tasting blood.

"I'm sorry," he said. "I had to."

I began inching over to the door but stopped when I saw the fierce, sudden step he took toward me.

"What?" I said.

"What brings you here?" he demanded.

"Mr. Archer," I said, feeling the tears spring to my eyes. "That's all. I just wanted to talk to Mr. Archer."

He smiled slightly, showing small white pointy teeth.

"I believe," he said, "Mr. Archer is busy. Keeping the wolves from the door."

Wolves?

And then I realized, or thought I realized: Mr. Archer was protecting him from the marshal, the bounty hunters, hiding him here.

And what about me now that I'd seen him? Who would protect me?

I started toward the door again, more slowly this time. I could outrun him. He wouldn't want to show himself.

"You won't say that you saw me," he said sharply.

"I won't," I whispered.

"Your word?" he said. "I have your promise?"

I could promise anything. To get safely away.

I nodded. "I promise." I backed farther toward door.

He pointed a finger. "You will be held to it," he said.

I nodded, then bent and gathered up my coat, which had fallen to the floor, and opened the door.

I looked over my shoulder at him, to be sure he

wasn't about to follow, then fled, letting the door slam behind me.

Once out of the room, I stood in the center of the store, my heart racing wildly, my mind racing, too. What to do? Where to go? I can't stay here!

I was standing there, breathing hard, when the front door opened and Mr. Archer came in, bundled against the cold, a huge muffler hanging almost to his knees.

His eyes widened when he saw me, surprised-looking. "Need something else?" he asked, his voice sharp, annoyed.

I swallowed. "Work," I said. "I came to work."

He put both hands to his head, pressing one on each temple as though he had a headache. "You're in school, aren't you?" he bellowed. "Get! Go!"

I couldn't help it. Maybe it was a reaction to what had just happened, a reaction to fear. But suddenly I was crying, big fat tears that just rolled down my face. "Brother Foster said I could!" I said. "You said —"

"After school!" he practically shouted at me. "I meant after school! There'll be plenty of work then. Go!" He pointed to the door. "Now!"

"I'm going," I said.

"Wait!" he said. "Don't come back today. I need you tomorrow. Not today!"

I didn't answer, didn't even care why he said tomorrow, not today. I struggled with my coat, got one sleeve twisted up around my lunch pail, fought to un-tangle it, then hurried out, my coat hanging half on, half off, one sleeve flapping loose behind me. I didn't turn to look behind me, to even say good-bye. I just fled. Away from that place. Away from that terrible, awful place.

ᦂ Chapter Eight ᦂ

That night I lay awake for a long time after Leila fell asleep, listening to the creaking and sighing of the house as it settled, staring at the ceiling. The room was very bright, the moon, as well as the ground cover of snow, making it extra light. The shadows of bare tree limbs played across the moonlit ceiling, the branches seeming to shiver as they swayed and creaked in the night wind.

I pulled the quilt tightly around my shoulders and snuggled close to Leila, shivering — with cold, with fear. I had barely stopped shivering since that morning, since what happened in the back of the store. At school, even Sarah had noticed, asking me if I was getting sick.

Did I dare go back there?

Who was the man?

An escaped slave. He had to be.

But he'll almost certainly be gone tomorrow, I thought, moved along to someplace safe.

I shuddered and pulled the covers more tightly about me. Then Leila too suddenly shifted, sighing loudly, as though she'd just had a sad thought or dream.

I turned, propped myself on one elbow, and looked down at her.

She didn't seem sad, just peaceful. She was taking soft, rapid breaths, and I wondered if she were dreaming her dream of flying. She often told me of that dream she had over and over again. She's a falcon, she says, flying over Papa's ship and guiding him out of the dangerous ice fields in the Arctic.

Such a free feeling it must be to fly.

I lay down again, snuggling close to her, thinking how hard this all was on her. But at least she had her dreams to help her, her visions.

Mama had her faith.

And me?

No faith. Except in myself. I could provide. And then the thought crept in, the one I'd been fighting all day: I could provide one hundred dollars.

Monstrous! I turned and buried my head under my pillow, just the way I used to do when I was a little girl and had a scary thought. Hiding like that didn't help, though. The words, the voice, pursued me: A hundred dollars would really help your family.

Yes, but I wouldn't do such a terrible thing.

I took the pillow off my head and sat up then, knowing sleep wasn't coming. I eased quietly out of bed, found my dressing gown, and wrapped it around me, then tiptoed over to the window.

I could see down to the harbor, hear, even through the closed window, the creaking and sighing as the masts swayed and bent in the night wind. The moon was bright, lighting up the snow and the ships, poking into the corners of the dock.

I saw a ship with a broken mast, lying crazily against another, as though leaning in close to talk.

From out of the dark, a cat came, stalking something, its shadow trailing along beside it, making it seem like a twin cat, a double. It leapt up onto the stone wall, crouched low, its tail straight out behind it, then crept along the stones and disappeared into the night.

A cloud raced across the moon, blocking out the light for a moment, making the ships and the harbor disappear. As the cloud lingered, all was black, and then the cloud was gone and the ships and harbor and even the cat were back.

And someone else.

A man. Pacing back and forth at the foot of the

hill, looking out to sea, then all around him, then back to sea, as though waiting for something.

What?

I bent, leaning closer to the glass, feeling the cold air move against my face. Who would be out at such an hour?

The watchman — Simon Joe, the night watchman! He had made it home safely. I breathed a sigh of relief, smiling. He was safe! And then I wondered: What must it be like to be a watchman, watching the harbor, keeping ships safe? It must feel good to take such good care of others.

I shivered and hurried back to bed, my feet suddenly icy cold against the floor. I curled myself into a little ball, and I must have slept, because suddenly I was being woken. Leila was sitting up beside me, the bed shaking.

"What?" I said. "What is it?"

"Oh, Gen!" she said, crying. "Gen!"

I sat up quickly. "What is it? Are you sick? Does something hurt? Where does it hurt?"

She leaned against me. "A dream!" She was sobbing now. "I had a bad dream, a horrible, scary dream."

I put my arms around her and held her close, feeling her small body shudder with sobs. "It's all right," I said softly. "It's all right. It was just a dream. It's all gone now."

She shook her head, still buried in my shoulder. "Not just a dream," she whispered.

"It's all right," I said. I held her away from me, then laid her gently down on the pillow and pulled the quilt up to her chin, tucking it tightly all around her. "Tell me," I said.

"That dream," she whispered. "The one about Papa. It was different, Gen."

"Tell me," I answered.

"I'm flying," she said. "High on winter's wind, just like always, and I'm looking for Papa's ship. I'm this huge bird, a falcon, and I —"

"Find him!" I said, smiling. "You always find him and lead him home."

"Yes!" she said. "But this time we're almost home, and right near our house, there's another bird, a snow goose. It flies right over our house and — and —"

"What?" I said.

"It's too late," she said, sobbing once again.

"Too late?" I said. "Too late for what?"

"For Mama — oh, Gen! It's too late for Mama. She's the snow goose, and she's lost! She flies far away from us, and we call her back and call her back, but she can't find her way back to us. And you, you were in trouble, too."

I felt my heart begin to pound hard. Mama! Mama

had been so strange, but she wasn't really lost to us, was she? What was this dream? A message? An omen?

I swallowed hard, making my voice sound more confident, firmer than I felt. "Listen, Leila," I said. "It was just a dream. Mama isn't lost, and I'm not in trouble."

Not much. Not now. Not yet.

Please, God.

"Just a dream," I repeated soothingly. "It was just a dream."

"Yes," she said. "But I'm scared."

"I know," I said back. "Dreams are like that sometimes."

Neither of us spoke for a while, as I continued to smooth her hair and pat her, continued to think of Mama. We couldn't lose Mama, too!

"What if Mama dies before Papa gets home?" Leila whispered after a while, echoing my own thought. "What will happen to us? Will they put us in an orphanage, like they did to Amanda and her baby sister?"

"No," I said firmly, lying down beside her and hugging her close to me, pulling the covers tightly around both of us. "Mama is not going to die, and we're not going to an orphanage. Amanda and her sister, that was different. Their papa just went crazy after their mama died. Mama's just a little strange. Sadness does that to people sometimes. But you don't die of sadness, Leila! Besides, I told you I have work. Tomorrow. Mr. Archer said come after school tomorrow — I told you that. We'll get Mama food and a doctor. She's going to be fine, Leila. And so will you. And so will I."

And that, I thought suddenly, was the truth. We will all be fine.

And if I have to turn myself into a bounty hunter to make sure of that, I will do that, too.

May God forgive me.

↫ Chapter Nine ↬

Next day in school, everyone was talking about slavery. There had been another riot in Boston, an escaped slave dragged through the streets to a ship that was waiting to take him back South. This time, though — different from the time with Anthony Burns — a crowd came out and rescued him from the marshals and chased off the federal troops. Also, there had been a meeting at Faneuil Hall, where even Mr. Thoreau had spoken, imploring people to take action against the Fugitive Slave Law. Boston is a long way away from New Bedford, but all the important things seem to happen there.

But there was one thing that eventually made everyone in school stop talking slavery — and even helped me to stop thinking about it for the moment. Mr. Hathaway was planning a recitation for New Year's

Night, where students could recite something they had prepared, such as a poem or a prayer or something they had written. Only the best students could do it, and Mr. Hathaway announced a contest for the best-prepared and best-delivered recitation. We had only a few weeks to practice and were starting that very day, with time allowed right then for us to talk and plan.

It sounded so exciting. First because we could all be out at night for the recital, like grown-ups. And then because we'd all be together on New Year's Night. That would be good because the holiday would probably be a little sad for Leila and Mama and me. Maybe we could even get Mama to come out with us, although I didn't really believe that. But Sarah would be there, and Edgar, too!

I looked at Sarah in the seat beside me, and she looked back, smiling at me, that sweet smile of hers. "We could do a poem together," she said, clasping her hands and resting her chin on them. "At Meeting once, Mrs. Walker, Mama's friend, she told Mama about how she and her twin sister did a poem for a recital when they were little, one saying one line, then one the next."

"It sounds nice," I said.

But I couldn't help thinking I'd like to do one of my own. Papa always told me what a pretty voice I had, and even though no one else said so, I rather thought so, too. Besides, I could say a beautiful poem, one that would make Edgar notice.

I sighed. Why did I think about him so much when I didn't even really like him?

"Do you want to?" Sarah said. "Do one together?"

"Maybe. Which poem?" I said.

"I'm not sure. Do you know any?"

I nodded. I knew many, mostly ones Papa used to recite for us, especially from the New Testament, which Papa always said was like poetry to him. Every Christmas, he would read the Magnificat to us, but I didn't know if I could ever say that prayer again, now that he was gone.

I looked around the room, looking for the literature book, the one with poetry in it. One of the girls, Emmaline Robbins, had already snatched it, and she and the twins Fannie and Jewel Martin were already busy turning pages, hogging the whole thing. Everyone else was bent over desks, whispering and planning, Leila with her best friend, Imogene, and Sam Block with Joke Daniels.

I saw Edgar staring down at his desk, a worried look on his face. I hadn't spoken to him since that day he'd walked us home, and I wondered what he'd thought about that day, what he was thinking about now that made him look so worried.

He looked up then, and I quick turned back to Sarah. "We could do 'A Summer's Garden,' " I said.

"That one we did at Commencement one year?" she asked.

I nodded.

"Too short," she said. "And boring. How about 'My Brother's Grave'?"

" 'My Brother's Grave'?" I said. "It's so long! And so sad!"

"Good!" she said. "We can be pitiful!"

She clasped her hands to her chest, her eyes rolled up, attempting — and achieving — a most pitiful look.

I shook my head. There was enough in the world to be pitiful about without choosing pitiful poetry. "No," I said. "I don't want to be pitiful."

"Oh, wait!" Sarah said suddenly, turning to me, her eyes troubled. "I wonder if I'll be allowed to do this."

"Allowed?" I said.

"Papa!" she said, pulling a face. "Papa won't let me act or be in tableaus or anything. Maybe he'll say this is like acting or theater."

"It's not, though," I said. "Besides, he let you do Commencement that time."

"That was different," she said. "That was school."

"This is school, too," I said. "Besides, there are other Quakers here. If they can do it, so can you. There's Edgar and his little brother. And Emma Badger and Judith."

She shrugged. "I don't know," she said.

We both looked over at Edgar then. He had raised his hand and was waiting for Mr. Hathaway to recognize him.

"I'll bet he's going to say the same thing," Sarah said softly.

Edgar must have realized we were looking at him, because after a minute, he turned to us. Turned to us and smiled at us. No, not at us. At me!

When he smiled, his whole face lit up, and even his eyes crinkled up. His green eyes. And how did I know they were green?

I looked away, feeling my heart pound hard, my face and ears get flaming hot.

Sarah leaned in close to me. "Genevieve's in love, Genevieve's in love," she whispered, her lips against my ear.

I poked her hard with my elbow, much harder than I'd intended to. "Hush up!" I said.

She jerked away from me and squealed, then quickly clapped a hand over her mouth.

Too late.

"That kind of behavior will guarantee that neither of you has a part, Miss Genevieve, Miss Sarah," Mr. Hathaway said.

"I'm sorry, Mr. Hathaway," I said, trying to look like I meant it.

"It was just an accident, Mr. Hathaway," Sarah said.

He raised his eyebrows but didn't say anything more.

When he turned to acknowledge Edgar's raised hand, I turned to Sarah. "I'm not sorry," I whispered.

She just grinned, her face deep red, trying to hold back a laugh.

I glared at her again, but she didn't even seem to care.

"Mr. Hathaway," Edgar said, "my brother Samuel and I maybe can't do this. The New Year is a special time to spend with our family."

"Correct," Mr. Hathaway said. "That's why everyone is invited."

"Yes, sir," Edgar said. "But I still don't know —"

"That your family would like to be there?" Mr. Hathaway interrupted.

Edgar shrugged, looking miserable. "It's not that, sir. I'm just not sure if my pa would —"

"You may be excused, then, if necessary," Mr. Hathaway said shortly, waving a hand, dismissing him. He looked around the room. "Anyone else?" he asked.

I looked at Sarah.

"I'll ask Papa first," she said softly. She bent her head and leaned in close to me. "Oh, what if he doesn't let me?"

"He will," I said, even though I wasn't sure. Besides, I wasn't sure I cared about the recital at all if

Edgar wasn't going to be there. And then I had a bad thought: Would I be able to be there, even if I wanted to be? That afternoon would be my first at the store — if I went there, and I was pretty sure I would. But because I'd be starting late after school, how long would they expect me to work? Maybe I'd have to work on New Year's Day? Part of the day, anyway?

Or would I?

Like maggots in spoiled meat, the thoughts crept back: Turn in the slave if he's still there. A hundred dollars. Work just until you find out where he's kept hidden. Then you'll surely be off on New Year's Day, with plenty of money in your pocket, too.

Hateful. You'd be as hateful as Joke Daniels.

Except even Joke wouldn't really turn in anyone.

"Sarah?" I said quietly. "Is there a difference between a swear and a promise?"

"Quakers don't swear," she said. "Not in court, not even when we get married."

"Oh," I said. "But is promising something as serious as swearing it?"

"We should always be true in word and deed, my father says. Why?" Her eyes got wide. "I know!" she said. "A secret! You have a secret. Something you promised not to tell."

Her eyes were dancing, just as they always do when she talks secrets.

But a hidden slave was not a secret I could share with her. Except then I thought about working after school. That was a secret, and I should tell her first, before she found out from someone else.

"I do have a sort of secret," I said quietly. "Everyone will know it soon, but I want to tell you first."

"What?" she said, leaning in close to me.

I looked around the room to be sure no one else was listening, then leaned closer to her again.

"I'm going to be working," I said. "I have a job."

"Working?" she said, pulling back and staring at me. "You're lying."

I grinned at her. "Quakers don't lie!" I said.

"You're not a Quaker," she said back.

"But I am working. I'm going to be working in Mr. Archer's store. Starting today."

"Only grown-ups have jobs," she said. "Or boys sometimes. Girls work only at home!"

"But not me," I said.

She shook her head. "I don't believe you."

I just shrugged.

"Well, how come?" she said. "I mean, why?"

I looked down at the desk, fiddled with my slate. "Because," I said, looking up at her at last. "We need it. Need the money."

"You need it?" she said. "But what about your —"

"Papa?" I interrupted. "Or Mama? You know

Papa's gone. And Mama is really sick, strange lately, with headaches and all. And Sarah, there's hardly any . . ."

But I couldn't tell her that, about there being no food. And no money. And no repairs to the house and no clothes — although that was probably becoming obvious to everyone — everyone besides Mama. Anyway, I'd already said too much.

I shrugged. "I just need to."

"And what have you girls prepared?"

It was Mr. Hathaway standing over us, his chubby cheeks flushed, rolls of flesh spilling over the collar of his shirt like fat pink worms. "I assume you're not wasting your time simply visiting?"

"Oh, no!" I said. "We're not. We were talking about 'My Brother's Grave' and —"

"A sentimental poem!" he said, waving a dismissive hand. "Don't do it. What else?"

What else?

I looked at Sarah and she at me.

She shrugged. Neither of us had been talking poems. So I said the one thing that popped into my head: "The Magnificat."

He frowned. "The what?"

"The Magnificat," I repeated. I took a deep breath. "You know: 'My soul doth magnify the Lord, and my spirit hath rejoiced in God my Savior. For He hath regarded the humility of His handmaid; for behold from henceforth all generations shall call me blessed —' "

I stopped, embarrassed. The words had come so easily, each word remembered, the way Papa used to read it to us in his deep, rich voice, each Advent season, and I suddenly ached for his voice again.

I looked down at my desk, feeling the red creep up my neck.

"It might do," Mr. Hathaway said. "Prepare it, and I'll hear the rest tomorrow."

He moved away then, to listen to Fannie and Jewel.

When he was gone, Sarah whispered, "That was beautiful."

Yes. But it made me lonely. And it made me sorrowful, too, not just for Papa, but for something else, something inside me, some belief or trust perhaps that I once had that was now missing.

"Gen?" Sarah said.

"What?"

"You know the rest of that Scripture?" she said.

I nodded. " 'He hath filled the hungry with good things,' " I said, " 'and the rich He hath sent empty away —' "

"Yes!" Sarah said, interrupting. "And Papa says that's what Quakers are supposed to do, do what He did. Papa recites that passage from Luke all the time."

Again I shrugged. It was a nice thought, a good thought. But God helps those who help themselves. And in spite of all my doubts, I was about to help myself and my family. One way or another.

⤳ Chapter Ten ⤳

After school that day, when Sarah and I parted at the alley in back, I hurried down the street to the store. I had decided not to think about whether there was anyone hidden there, about whether Mr. Archer knew I knew about anything. I would just go there and see what happened. And most important, I wouldn't say anything unless Mr. Archer said anything. I still hadn't decided definitely what I'd do if it was — or had been — an escaped slave back there, although a plan was forming in the back of my head.

I did worry about that back room, though, wondered how I'd feel going in there.

Scared probably. Very scared.

I hurried along the street, stepping around people bustling here and there, merchants and newsboys and people out visiting or going on errands, all of them seeming happy to be outdoors after being snowed in for so long.

When I got to the store, I went in, trying to make myself do what Mama used to tell us to do — back when Mama was still talking and acting normally. She used to tell us, when it was hot out in summer for example, that if we acted as though we were cool, we'd feel cool.

Maybe if I could act calm, I'd feel calm?

I took a few deep breaths, then opened the door and went in.

Mr. Archer was behind the long counter that runs the length of the room, waiting on a woman customer with a long shopping list in her hand. He looked up at me when I came in.

"Hang your coat in back!" he called out cheerfully, not at all in that grouchy way he'd had the other morning. "And then take the duster to the shelves back there. I'll be with you shortly."

I nodded.

The woman at the counter turned and stared at me. I didn't recognize her, although from the old-fashioned way she was dressed and the way her coat had been mended many times, I was quite sure that she was a maid from up on the hill. She looked me slowly up and down, as though she were measuring me.

I looked right back at her, my chin high. You work, I work, I told her silently.

I turned toward the back then, my heart beginning to thump uncomfortably hard.

Silly. As though Mr. Archer would let someone be hiding there, when he told me to go back there.

Still, when I went into the room, I had to take a quick look behind the door before I closed it behind me. But of course there was no one.

Once inside, I stood in the center of the room, looking around. It was a big room, piled high with cartons and crates stacked on shelves as well as piled every which way on the floor. There were a table and chairs, too, the tabletop also littered with boxes and some big ledger books.

I went over to the shelves and looked at the boxes. They held every kind of thing I could imagine: string and nails and tacks and screws. There were tins of flour and oatmeal, and salt and sugar. There were sewing supplies and bolts of cloth, shovels and hammers and picks. Practically every item a town could need was stored in this room, all the things a human being could need.

Mama and Leila and I would never go hungry if I owned a place like this!

Thinking of Mama made me wonder how Leila was doing with her, if Mama would notice that I was late coming home. All I could do was pray that it would be all right.

I hung up my coat and looked around for the duster Mr. Archer had mentioned, then found it lying on the table next to an old oily rag. I picked them both up, then looked around once more.

It was clear this place needed dusting, maybe more than dusting. It was really dirty. And cleaning was one thing I knew how to do: You just take something that's dirty, and you rub and scrub it till it comes clean.

I gathered up my skirts, climbed up on a step stool that was propped against a shelf, and began my work. I began with the top shelf — something I'd learned from our housekeeper, Martha, before we'd had to let her go, that one always started at the top and worked down — although why I didn't know.

The dust was thick up there, a greasy kind of dust, and I made a plan as I set about working: Pick up each item, clean it, clean under it, put it back.

Once I'd done each item within reach, I climbed down, moved the step stool again, and climbed back up.

It wasn't exactly fun, but it was a satisfying feeling. Things were getting clean, and I'd be getting paid.

But how much?

We hadn't talked about that part at all.

I had just finished another section of the top shelf when the door opened and Mr. Archer came in.

He smiled up at me, rather a surprised kind of smile. "You seem to know what you're doing," he said, nodding approvingly.

"I do," I said. And then realized that perhaps that sounded a little conceited, so I added, "It's really awfully dirty." And then realized that sounded even worse.

I blushed and turned back to the shelf.

Mr. Archer just laughed, though. "It *is* dirty!" he said. "I don't believe it's been touched in a year or more. But that's one of the things we hired you for."

"What else?" I said, because I thought this was as good a time as any to ask about my duties, as well as my pay.

"Come down from there, and we'll discuss it," Mr. Archer said.

I gathered up my skirts in one hand and used the other to steady myself against the shelves as I came down from my perch.

Once down off the step stool, I followed him over to the cluttered table where the books and boxes were piled. Three chairs were placed haphazardly around the table, and Mr. Archer sat heavily in one. He's not exactly fat, just a little pudgy, but he always seems to be a bit out of breath.

"Sit!" he said, sighing and waving to a chair. "It feels good."

I sat in the chair farthest from him, my hands in my lap.

He opened a ledger, looked inside it, then looked over at me. "Tell me," he said, closing the book, "can you work three hours a day? Will that interfere with your schoolwork?"

I shook my head. "No," I said. "No, it won't."

"You can work every school day?"

I nodded. "Saturday, too?" I asked, because Saturday was a half day of school.

He shook his head no. "Not Saturday," he said. "Just Monday to Friday?"

"I can do that," I said.

But could I make enough money in just those few days, few hours?

I looked at him, waiting. How much? But he didn't seem to realize what I was waiting for.

"We'll start by cleaning first," he said. "You can bring this back room to some semblance of order. I haven't any daughters, but I understand that girls are good at that."

Girls are good at lots of things. But of course, I didn't say that out loud.

"And come summer," he continued, "I'll expect you to bring in supplies and perhaps make deliveries. Are you strong?"

"I'm strong," I said.

He frowned. "I won't be easy on you. I'll expect you to work every bit as hard as any boy would work."

This time, I couldn't help saying it, even though I knew it was bold. "I'm as good as any boy," I said.

"We'll give you a chance to prove it!" he said. "And if you do, we'll pay you a fair wage. Brother Foster thought a dollar a week to start would be fair. How does that sound to you?"

A dollar a week! That was a — a fortune! Too much. I looked at him and suddenly felt my eyes fill with tears.

I looked down at the table, blinking hard, then up at the ceiling, willing the tears not to run down my face.

A dollar a week. I couldn't possibly take a dollar a week for just three hours a day — fifteen hours a week!

"It's all I can afford for now," Mr. Archer said, worried-sounding, and I knew he had misread my tears. "But perhaps come summer we can do better."

"But you don't understand!" I said, finally looking at him. "It's too much. I mean, I can't take that much money. I can't work enough to justify that."

He laughed, a booming, hearty laugh, just as Brother Foster had done the other day. "Yes, you can!" he said. "You'll be working for it. Believe me, you'll be working for it."

I looked away from him again, taking deep breaths, calming myself, trying to find just the right words. Finally, after what seemed like minutes and minutes of silence, I said, "If you pay me that much, then you can keep half and I'll keep half. That way we can pay off what we owe you."

He shook his head and waved a hand, smiling slightly. "Don't worry about that," he said. "We'll think about that some other time. Now, let's get down to the rules. First, I expect you to work hard, a fair day's pay for a fair day's work. Also, I expect you to be prompt. And I trust that you'll keep my business to yourself. Understood?"

"Yes," I said, although I wasn't exactly sure I understood about keeping his business to myself.

"I mean," he added, as though reading my thoughts, "there are business matters that are private. They should remain private. Not spoken of to anyone."

Like a slave, a hidden slave? I didn't dare look at him.

"Everything you see here stays here," he went on. "Anything you hear here does not get repeated. I have your promise about that?"

I kept looking down at the tabletop. Promise? But what if I had to tell about the slave? What if I needed to collect that hundred dollars?

There was a long silence, one that seemed to stretch

on and on, until Mr. Archer said softly, "Brother Foster seemed to think you could be trusted. If you can't — can't promise that — you should go home now."

"Oh, I can!" I said, looking up at him quickly. "I can be trusted. Really, I can!"

"Then I have your promise?" he said.

I nodded. "You have my promise," I said.

And even though I knew it was foolish, childish even, I kept my fingers under the tabletop firmly crossed.

⌒ Chapter Eleven ⌒

All is well. That was Papa's favorite saying. He'd say it in summer on our nighttime walks as we stood by the ocean, looking up at the sky. He'd say it in winter when we sat inside rooms warmed by the fire, watching snow fall outside. He'd say it especially often in the letters he used to write, letters sent on by the cargo ships, promising us that all was well and that he would return to us. *All is well,* he'd write at the end of each letter. All is well.

All was not well with us. Not completely well. But as Christmas approached, some of it was better, mostly because we had food, plenty enough to eat, and it took some worry away from my mind. I was especially relieved to know that Leila was getting enough food to pad out those tiny bird bones of hers. Also, nobody had come to tell Mama what I was doing. And I hadn't seen any more escaped slaves in the store.

Things were better.

Except for Mama. She seemed to live more and more inside her own head, whispering to herself sometimes, noticing little of what went on around her, not even noticing that I came home well after dark each day. One day when Leila had come home from school, she'd found Mama, scissors in hand, sitting on the floor by Papa's old sea chest. Mama had cut up everything that was in the chest — a picture of Papa, letters from Papa's old voyages, some silk ribbons Papa had once brought home, postcards with pictures on them. Leila said things were in tatters and shreds all around the room. I hadn't seen it, because Leila had cleaned it all up before I got home. But since then, Leila and I had hidden all the scissors in the house.

I was working on a plan, though, for helping Mama. Each week when I got paid, I walked around the store, choosing food for the week and trying to select one special delicacy that might restore Mama's health and make her happy again. I was also saving a penny or two each week for the time when we called on the doctor. I knew that he'd see Mama anyway, pay or no pay, but afterward he'd surely send a bill. It was important to me to have the money to pay that bill.

On the Friday of my third week of work, the week before Christmas, I chose an orange as Mama's special treat. I didn't put the orange in the sack with the other groceries, though, because I was afraid it would get squashed. Instead I laid it carefully, wrapped in tissue, in a small box on the shelf in the back room till it was time to go home.

I felt happy that day, even hopeful. Friday was always such a good day, with money in my pocket and food in a sack, ready to take home. And Saturday and Sunday were coming, time to catch up on my studies and time to spend with Mama, to try and bring her out of her reverie.

When I finished my work that day, I hung up my apron in back, put on my coat, and got my sack of groceries. I went out the front way, saying good night to Mr. Archer as I passed. He had already turned down the gas lamp in front and was standing in the half dark, totaling up the day's receipts.

He nodded to me and murmured good night.

Outside, I closed the door behind me and stood on the walkway a moment, taking deep breaths of the night air. It was a beautiful night, cold and clear and bright with stars.

I crossed the street and paused a moment before starting up the hill, looking out toward the sea.

I shifted the sack, hugging it close to me for warmth, and turned my face upward to the sky. As I watched, suddenly a star blazed across the sky east to west, a streak of magical falling star that plummeted from sight as suddenly as it had appeared.

Star light, star bright.

I wish I may, I wish I might . . .

What would I wish for, if stars could grant wishes? For Mama to be better. For Papa to be alive. For gifts in our Christmas stockings.

Gifts! An orange, Papa used to give us. I had forgotten Mama's orange, forgotten to put it in the sack!

I turned and hurried back across the street.

Foolish me, daydreaming about falling stars when Mama's treat was back there in the store.

I hurried along the wooden sidewalk, hoping I'd get to the store before Mr. Archer locked up for the night. When I got there, though, it was totally dark, all the lights already turned out.

Now what? I tried the door anyway, and to my surprise, the knob turned.

I opened it and went in, calling out as I did. "Mr. Archer? Mr. Archer, are you here?"

No answer.

The only light in the room came from the gas lamp outside the window.

Odd, to find the door unlocked. Mr. Archer must have gone out the back way, across the alley to his house, forgetting to lock up the front.

I sighed. I'd have to go back there and tell him to come and lock up. Well, I'd do it, but first my orange.

Slowly, carefully, I made my way across the store toward the back. It was practically pitch black, but I knew my way fairly well. Besides, after a minute, once my eyes became accustomed to the dark, I could see enough, at least enough not to trip over anything.

I managed to get to the back room door, then reached to open it.

And remembered my first day there.

Silly. You've worked here three weeks and seen nothing, nobody.

I took a deep breath, opened the door, and went in — and couldn't help taking a look behind the door all the same.

No one. Not even a shadow.

It was awfully dark in the room, though, even darker than the front. I could tell more by the feel than anything else where things were. Carefully, one hand outstretched, I made my way to the table, put down the sack, then turned and groped for the shelf.

I had to fumble a little but found it at last — the shelf, the small box, the orange.

I turned, picked up the sack from the table where I'd put it, then dropped the orange in its box carefully down inside.

I turned back then and stood for a minute at the window that faced the back alley, peering out, thinking. Mr. Archer would definitely have to come back and lock up. Should I go out the back way, across the alley to his house, or around by way of the front?

No lights out there in back, none at all. I'd go out the front, then around by way of the wooden walkway along the side of the store. That way, I could at least feel my way in the dark, feel the boards under my feet.

I turned back from the window, the sack clutched firmly in both hands.

Turned.

And saw him.

The man.

A man.

Someone crouched in a corner of the room.

The fear was so sudden and icy inside, that for a moment I didn't move. Couldn't move. Couldn't breathe.

Then my hand flew to my throat, and unknowing, I let the sack fall to the floor. There was a horrendous sound. A jar rolled, bumped, hit against the wall. Then was still.

The man lunged toward me. "My God, my God!" he cried, stopping no more than a foot away from me. "Why hast Thou forsaken me?"

I stepped back and he leaned farther toward me, his neck twisted sideways to look at me, as though his back or neck was stiff with pain.

I tried to speak — opened my mouth — but no sound came out.

I stared.

The man stared back.

He began to straighten up.

Paralyzed. I was paralyzed, stiff with fear.

All I could think was he'd put his hand on my mouth. So I did it myself, covered my mouth with my hand.

He stood up fully then, his eyes fixed on mine.

Not the man I'd seen before. A different man. Older. But a Negro.

He didn't move any farther, not toward me, not away. Just stayed there — still, his arms slightly away from his sides.

I knew him. Not his name. But I knew he was, had to be, a slave. An escaped slave.

"Lord!" the man cried out again, his voice hoarse and wild, but strangely soft, too, as though crying out in a whisper. "They have slain Thy prophets, they have razed Thy altars, and I only am left, and they are seeking my life. Why, Lord, why?"

What to do?

Scream? Call for Mr. Archer? Run?

Yes. But I stood dumbly, staring.

"Why, Lord, why?" he continued. He turned his eyes to the ceiling, lifted his hands, gesturing, as though in real conversation with the Lord. "They all seek my life, don't you see? Now even the children seek it."

For a moment, his eyes stayed fixed on the ceiling,

a pleading kind of look, as though waiting for an answer, then slowly, slowly, he began rocking himself to and fro, to and fro.

There was a long silence, while my heart thudded hard against my ribs.

Should I run? He was old. I could outrun him. Twist. Turn. Like a deer, chased by a wolf pack. He wouldn't be able to follow.

His eyes turned to me, cold hard eyes.

I backed up a step. "Who are you?" I whispered. "What are you doing here?"

"What does it matter who I am?" he said. "Perhaps that should be my name. Matter. What does it Matter? It doesn't Matter."

He sighed and closed his eyes for a second, then opened them. "Israel," he said softly. "Israel's my name."

"But why are you . . . ?"

I didn't finish.

There was another long silence while he watched me closely, his eyes narrowed, as though he were thinking.

I thought, too. I could be away in no time. I knew the layout of the store, knew the way to the front.

But then I'd have to leave our food, Mama's orange.

"Why are you here now?" he asked quietly.

"Mama's orange," I said. "I forgot my mama's orange. She needs it."

"Needs it? She's ill, your mama?" he asked.

"Yes," I said.

"I'm sorry," he said.

I began inching toward the door. "Yes, and I have to go now," I said. "I'll get my food and —"

"Wait!" His voice was soft, but he stepped in front of me, and there was no doubt that he didn't mean to let me go.

"Mama needs me," I said, feeling suddenly as if I were about to cry. "My sister expects me."

"You'll go soon," he said. "But I don't know yet if you're friend or foe."

I didn't know, either. One hundred dollars. Two years' work.

A light suddenly appeared outside the back window, a moving, swirling light, the kind of light made by someone swinging a lantern.

I looked at the man Israel, and he looked back at me. He didn't shrink back against the wall, though, hiding or crouching as I'd have expected him to.

Instead he watched the progress of the light as it came right up to the back window, the back door. I could feel my heart beating furiously in my throat as I held my breath and watched, too, my eyes fastened on the doorknob as it slowly turned.

Mr. Archer? Another escaped slave? Someone else? I could hardly bear the pounding beat of my heart as the door swung inward. And Brother Foster stepped into the room. Brother Foster, bringing in cold air, bringing in a lantern and light.

He looked from one of us to the other, then back.

"Miss Genevieve!" he said finally, his voice loaded with surprise — or was it anger? "What are you doing here?"

"Is she a friend, Brother?" Israel asked. "Or foe?"

"Friend," Brother Foster answered without a pause, without even looking at me. "She is a friend."

Chapter Twelve

Leila was waiting for me when I ran up onto the porch that night, waiting just inside the front door, her nose pressed hard against the glass pane.

When she saw me come up on the porch, she flung open the door, stepped out, and threw her arms around me. "Oh, Gen!" she cried. "I'm so glad you're home."

"What is it?" I asked, looking down at her.

She held tight to me, trembling.

"Mama?" I asked, fear clutching at my stomach.

She shook her head. "No, you!" she said, looking up at me, her eyes dark with fear. "I was so scared for you."

I untangled her arms from around me, then urged her ahead of me into the house and closed the door behind us. "I'm just a little late," I said. "No need to get all agitated."

I headed down the hall toward the kitchen.

I was so frightened still. I needed time alone, time to think. But Leila followed me.

"I'm not agitated," she said from behind me. "Just worried. I worry about you a lot."

"Too much," I said.

"What happened?" she asked when we got to the kitchen.

What happened?

They all seek my life, don't you see? Now even the children seek it.

"She is a friend," Brother Foster had said. He hadn't even reminded me of my promise to Mr. Archer not to tell anything that went on in the store. He had simply helped me pick up my groceries, seen me to the front door, and said, "Good night, friend."

"Gen?" Leila said.

"What?"

"I asked you. What happened? I had such a strong sense of trouble. It happened once before, too, when you went there, but —"

"No trouble!" I said. "Now, stop being dramatic. Nothing happened." I began taking groceries out of the sack and putting them into cupboards and bins. "I just forgot to pick up my things at the store when I left — that's all. I had to go back and get them."

And had Brother Foster been using the word *friend*

the way Quakers do, meaning I was one of them, a Friend?

I wasn't one of them. I wasn't one of anybody. I didn't want to be one of anybody. I didn't want to be — I couldn't be — the person Brother Foster thought I was.

Quietly then, I set about preparing dinner — beans, brown bread, and relish — my mind racing, worrying.

Another escaped slave.

Was this another opportunity?

"Gen?" Leila said.

"What?" I answered.

"You're being awfully quiet," she said.

I shrugged. "Sometimes I am," I said.

"Why?" she said.

"Just because I am!" I said, my words coming out much more impatiently than I'd meant them to.

"Well, you're being a mean thing!" she said.

I shrugged. "So sometimes I'm a mean thing," I answered.

"Then I won't tell you my secret!" she said.

"What secret?" I said.

I looked across the room at her.

She had moved from the table over to the stove and was standing there, her arms folded across her chest, backed against the stove for warmth. Her bottom lip was thrust out in a pout, her eyes wide as if

she were about to cry. She looked so thin, so cold —
so young! — her arms wrapped tightly around herself like that, trying to warm herself, fighting back
tears.

It was nonsensical, but suddenly I felt as if I, too,
were about to cry.

I looked away from her and out the window.

It had begun to snow, a soft, gentle kind of snow.
Odd, just an hour ago, the stars were out and the
moon shone brightly.

So much changed, so fast.

All is well. Then all is not well.

A hundred dollars had appeared again.

A hundred dollars against a life?

Yes, a hundred dollars against a life. Our life.

Then what kind of person have you become?

I sighed. One whom Brother Foster trusted.

I looked across the packed field of snow outside,
looked across to Sarah's house.

There were lights in the kitchen, flickering lights
in the rooms upstairs. It all looked so warm, so cozy.

All because a papa lived there?

I had to be the papa in this house, the mama, too.

I turned back to Leila. "What is it?" I said. "Tell me
your secret. I didn't mean to be short with you."

She looked up at me, her lips still in a huge pout.
"You're mean," she said.

I nodded. "Sometimes I am," I said. "But I don't intend to be. So tell me."

"You won't get angry?" she said.

I smiled. "I won't get angry," I said.

She looked down at the floor, turning the toe of her shoe round and round. "Promise?" she said.

"I promise," I said, and I made a little cross over my heart.

I moved back to the stove, stood alongside her. I lifted the lid of the bean pot and stirred a bit.

"I was listening before," Leila whispered, leaning against me. "And I heard something. I heard from Papa — I mean, I heard about Papa. It's why I was so anxious for you to get home."

"Papa?" I said. "What do you mean, heard from him?"

"We'll know something soon," she said. "A letter is on the way."

"From Papa?" I said.

She nodded and looked up at me, that wistful, hopeful look in her eyes that she would get whenever she talked about Papa, hoping that I'd believe, too.

I just shook my head. I had heard her imaginings far too many times before to believe. Yet I couldn't help realizing that this was the first time she'd been so specific. A letter?

I smiled at her, then put both my hands on her small shoulders, pushing her gently away from the stove so I could put in more wood. "I hope you're right, Leila," I said.

"You don't believe me, do you?" she said. "But I'm right. I really am."

"I hope so," I said again.

"Gen?" she said.

"What?" I said.

"Please believe? It's true. He's been in some kind of trouble — I don't know what, but it's better now and he can write to us, don't you see?"

I nodded at her but didn't answer.

"Gen?" she said after a minute. "Will you tell me the truth about something?"

"If I can," I said.

"Something scared you today, didn't it?" she said.

"Scared me?" I said, trying to sound surprised, yet feeling my heart begin its heavy thudding again. "Where did you get that idea?"

She shrugged. "I just did. And you know what, Gen? I'm scared, too."

I bent over the stove and put in more wood. "Scared of what?" I asked. "Something about Papa?"

"No," she said.

I straightened up and looked at her, saw her watching me, her eyes wide, as though she were really scared, just as she'd said. But it was strange the way she was watching me. She wasn't afraid of *me*, was she?

"What?" I said.

109

She looked down at her shoes. "You wouldn't do anything . . . anything bad, would you?" she said.

I brushed the wood bits from my hands, wiped my hands on my skirt, and put the lid back on the stove again. "Bad?" I said. "Like what?"

She shrugged. "I don't know. Just bad. Evil."

"I don't do bad or evil things," I said quietly. "Not if I can help it."

"But you have to help it!" she said urgently, grasping my hand. "You have to. You have to do what you know is right."

I pulled my hand out of hers, glared at her. What nerve, what gall, telling me what I should do! There in the warm kitchen, she had no fears, no worries — well, that wasn't true, she had plenty of fears and worries. But I was doing it all; I was taking care of her, caring for Mama, too, trying to keep Mama from going mad.

I turned away from her. See how well you can rescue this family, I wanted to say. See if you can do that and keep to your precious values. You're as bad as Brother Foster.

Suddenly I wanted to leave there, leave them to fend for themselves.

Instead I turned back to the stove and lifted the heavy lid of the bean pot. I stirred, tasted, salted it a bit, stirred again.

"Gen?" Leila said.

"Yes?" I answered.

"I didn't mean anything," she said. "I know you're a good, a very good, person."

I took a deep breath. "Go call Mama," I said gently. "Tell her her supper is waiting."

❧ Chapter Thirteen ❧

Time was a laggard that week, creeping, inching forward, me worrying, Mama sitting and staring, Leila
anxiously awaiting the letter from Papa. Foolish Leila
had actually taken to sitting by the parlor window beside Mama every minute she could, scanning the horizon, as if expecting the letter to swoop down from
the sky on seagull wings.

I had no patience with her, none at all. But I
seemed to catch some of her anxiety anyway, as worrisome, unsettling thoughts crowded in, like rat feet
scrabbling across an attic floor. Israel, the escaped
slave. I hadn't seen him again. There was no one in
the back room of the store. Yet I knew that didn't
make any difference, that one could still go to the
federal marshal and tell about the hiding place. All
the marshal would have to do was wait. Sooner or

later, he'd find someone, just as I had. And there would be a reward.

But I couldn't do it now. I didn't think I could do it now.

Because Brother Foster trusted me? Because Leila counted on me?

I wasn't sure, but it made my head ache just thinking about it. I also worried about something else, something maybe foolish that I had done, that I hadn't even told Leila about. One day after school, when I'd arrived at Mr. Archer's store, I saw a cart outside, loaded with lumber. When I went in, I found Brother Foster and some of his tall sons there, warming themselves around the fire, along with Sarah's papa and her big brother. They had been rebuilding a friend's barn roof that had been damaged in a fire, and the material in the cart was left over — at least, that's what they said. Could they use it to help repair our roof, our broken shingles? It would go to waste, otherwise, they said.

I could feel the heat come up my face.

"No, thank you!" I said.

Mr. Archer started to argue, but I glared at him, a fierce look such as I have never given any grown-up before, and he just nodded and sent the men away.

I worried, though. That was foolish of me, wasn't it? The house was awfully cold, the window still not repaired, the roof leaking. But I was taking care of my family. God helps those who help themselves.

I decided that I should stop worrying, that there were things to look forward to. Christmas Eve there was to be a dinner at Brother Foster's home, to which we'd all been invited, Mama and Leila, too. Mama of course refused to go, and Leila didn't want to, either, said that it would be boring, but I thought it was probably because she wanted to sit by the window and stare. I planned to go, if it felt right come Christmas Eve, mostly because Sarah was going. And Edgar, too. Mr. Archer was taking friends from town in his horse and buggy and had invited me to go with them. There was also the recitation on New Year's Night to look forward to. I had prepared the Magnificat, Sarah and me both. I hadn't wanted to do it for several reasons — first because it reminded me too much of Papa, and second because it seemed such a sham, a fake. How could I say that my soul magnified the Lord, that I rejoiced in His coming, believed in His mercy, when I didn't at all? When I believed only in me?

Yet Mr. Hathaway had set his mind on us doing it, so we had little choice. And maybe it was proud to say, but even though I didn't want to do it, I thought we did it awfully well when we practiced.

On Christmas Eve morning, I woke early, long before the sun was up, just the way I used to when I was little. I lay there staring out the window, watching the stars fade and morning begin to streak across the sky.

Thinking.

I looked down at Leila, asleep beside me still, her breath coming in soft little puffs, that peaceful look on her face that she has so often in sleep. Of what was she dreaming? Papa? She was so sure he was coming back, so sure of some mysterious letter.

But how will it get here, Leila? I asked her silently. No one has spotted his ship in years. Probably he isn't even alive, Leila. And I'm sorry for that. Sorry for you.

I got up, lit the fire, dressed for the day. There was no school that day, but there were plenty of chores to be done. Besides, I had some small gifts for Mama and Leila, and this would be a good time to wrap them. I had saved a few cents from each week's pay and bought two fine linen handkerchiefs for Mama, and on Saturday and Sunday afternoons, when Mama was napping, I'd embroidered little violets on the hems of each one. For Leila, I had two presents, a pad of drawing paper and a toy, a little man that danced at the end of a stick when you jiggled the stick up and down. I wasn't sure she'd want the toy, thought she'd probably want the drawing paper more, but I also knew she hadn't had a new toy in a very long time, so I'd bought it for her anyway.

Outside the window, the dawn was brighter, and I could hear birds waking up, sparrows and chickadees and snowbirds, as I went downstairs to start the fires for the day.

It took me a long time to get the fire going in the parlor and then in the kitchen. While I waited for the kitchen fire to be hot and for the kettle to boil, I laid the table for breakfast. That done, I used the time alone to wrap Leila's and Mama's presents. There was some old tissue paper Mama used to wrap up silks and woolens during the summer months, and I took some of that, and some silk ribbons that had made their way into a cupboard in the kitchen, and wrapped the three presents, using up all the ribbons, so that they looked very gay, very Christmasy.

When I was finished, I stood back and looked at them — bright ribbons, rustly white paper. Yes, they looked like Christmas. Not like Christmases of long ago — too few for that — but Christmas all the same.

I took the packages to the parlor to hide them. And was surprised to see Leila, already at the window, dressed, her hair brushed and shining, leaning forward, her hands on the windowsill.

She hadn't heard me come in, and I slipped the presents onto the floor and under a skirted table before I spoke.

"Leila?" I said.

She turned to me, startled but smiling. "I didn't hear you come in," she said.

I just shook my head. "I know you didn't," I said. "Still looking?"

She smiled. "You promised you wouldn't be angry," she said.

"I'm not angry," I said.

"It's almost Christmas," she said.

I couldn't help smiling at her. "I know," I said.

"And I have a present for you," she said, clasping her hands together in front of her. "A wonderful present."

"Really?" I said.

She nodded. "Yes. A drawing, I made you a wonderful drawing of a bird."

I laughed. "You're supposed to keep it a secret," I said.

She shrugged. "It is a secret. You haven't seen it yet. And know what? I made a drawing for Mama, too."

And then, as if the mention of her name had summoned her up, Mama suddenly appeared in the doorway from the hall. She wasn't dressed for the day, was still in her worn blue dressing gown, her hair undone and streaming around her shoulders, tangled from sleep.

She came into the room, walking right past us, as though she didn't even see us.

"Good morning, Mama," I said.

She didn't answer, just crossed the room to the window and sank heavily into her chair, her eyes already focused on the harbor and sea outside the window.

Leila looked at me, and I at her.

"Mama?" Leila said softly. "Are you all right?"

Mama didn't answer.

I crossed the room, stood beside Mama, reached down and took her hand.

"Good morning, Mama. How did you sleep?" I asked her softly.

Still no answer. Her hand lay cold in mine, cold and so limp it felt almost boneless.

"Mama!" I could feel the panic rising in my voice, and I fought it down. "Mama?" I said more softly, bending over her, looking into her face. "Can I get you something? Some tea?"

Her eyes were blank, wide and blank, as though she were seeing nothing. Not me, not anything, it seemed.

"What is it, Mama?" I said. "Does anything hurt?"

Her hands were freezing, and I rubbed them between my own, trying to warm them.

After a moment, I lowered them slowly to her lap and looked across her head to Leila. Leila's eyes met mine, hers dark, terrified almost, and in that instant, I thought I knew exactly what she was thinking: her dream. The snow goose, lost in her night sky.

"I'll go make Mama some tea," I said to Leila. "I put the water on before."

I looked back at Mama, her eyes fixed straight ahead, hands limp and cold in her lap.

"I'll get you tea, Mama," I said, bending close to her. "You'll be better in no time. You wait and see. Leila and I will take care of you."

I hurried from the room to the kitchen to prepare her hot drink.

But Leila's dream words followed me down the hall: What if it's too late, as she had said? What if Mama dies before Papa gets home?

She can't die, Leila.

Yes, but she doesn't even know it's Christmas. She doesn't see us. She doesn't even know who we are.

How will she even recognize Papa?

⮞ Chapter Fourteen ⮜

In spite of Mama's illness, I did go to Brother Foster's house that night, Chistmas Eve night. I went because Leila insisted I go and promised that she would come for me if Mama got worse. Also, as the day wore on, I could see that Mama was a little better. Leila and I had persuaded her to let us brush her hair and help her dress, and she had even eaten a little meal at noon. She still hadn't spoken all day, although by afternoon she had nodded in response to questions, as though she finally realized we were there.

Partly I felt guilty about going and leaving Leila. Partly I was relieved, happy to be out and away from that place, happy to be where Edgar was going to be. Still, all the way to Brother Foster's house, I kept my hands tucked under the carriage robe, my fingers tightly crossed. I knew it was silly — knew that wishing for luck didn't bring luck — but I did it all the same.

When we got to the Fosters' house, Mr. Archer helped his wife down from the carriage and then helped me down. There were three other carriages in the drive, and I saw some of Brother Foster's sons in their wide, awkward-looking hats, unhitching the horses and leading them to the barn, to keep them warm, I knew.

It was a bitter cold night, and after one of the boys returned from the barn and took our horses, we walked up to the house, the snow crunching beneath our feet, the stars shining brilliantly above us in the black sky. Against the horizon, I could see the outlines of trees, hear them whispering, rubbing their bare branches together in the cold night wind.

The front door stood open and the light streamed out onto the snow, and I couldn't help thinking how different it all was from home. Brother Foster's wife stood in the doorway, still greeting the guests who had arrived just before us. Behind her stood one of her sons, taking coats and wraps and blankets to put them by the fire to warm for when it was time to leave.

When Mrs. Foster greeted me, her eyes were warm.

"I have heard much about thee," she said, taking both my hands in her red chapped ones and pulling me inside the house. "Thou art a courageous lass."

I could feel my face get hot. "Not really," I said, feeling so shy suddenly that my voice was barely a whisper.

"Oh, yes," she said. "I don't know many who would do what thou has done. With nary a complaint. Thy mama must be very proud of thee."

My mama doesn't know.

Mrs. Foster continued to hold tightly to my hands, and I knew I was expected to answer. But looking into her kind, warm eyes, I couldn't think of one single thing to say.

"If I had a daughter," she went on, "I'd feel blessed if she were like thee."

I'd like a mama like you, I thought. But I only managed to whisper, "Thank you."

Mrs. Foster let go of my hands then, after first patting them gently, and I gave my coat to her son, then turned and looked around me.

Never have I seen a house so grand. Our house had once been grand, but never, never like this, not in the same way. People said Quakers lived simply — and maybe they did. But compared to the way we'd been living lately, this house was like a fairy-tale house.

In the center of this huge great-room was the biggest fireplace I'd ever seen. I could take our own hearth from our parlor and the dining room hearth, too, and put them right inside this one, and they would fit with room to spare. Suspended over the fire was a huge spit with a whole pig roasting on it. On one side of the room was a long, long table, as long as a church pew practically, covered with a white cloth and laden with food and things to drink.

There was a roasted turkey and an enormous ham, bowls of mashed potatoes and sweet potatoes, cranberry relishes and sweetmeats and pitchers of cider. On another table, at a right angle to the first one, were desserts — pies and cakes and a huge stollen filled with nuts and pieces of dried fruit.

I had never seen so much food in one place in my entire life. I couldn't help thinking of that night when Mama opened up the dining room — all the fancy plates, with no food on them at all. This much food would feed Mama and Leila and me for the whole winter!

In a corner of the room were a huge loom and a table for carding and spinning. Their very own loom! Hardly anyone was rich enough to have their own loom.

No wonder Brother Foster was so generous with my pay. And that thought made my face hot with shame. Wealthy people could still be stingy people. And Brother Foster was not stingy.

I must have been gaping at it all when someone grabbed my arm, and I turned to see Sarah, Sarah in her best Sunday dress, blue with a wide, white collar, and peeking out from beneath her dress, new shiny boots.

I didn't mean to feel jealous, but I found myself tucking my own feet under my dress.

"Merry Christmas, Gen!" Sarah said.

"Merry Christmas to you!" I said.

"Where's Leila?" Sarah said. "Didn't she come?"

I shook my head. "She's staying home with Mama. Mama's a little ill today."

"Well, you can bring her home some food, some treats!" Sarah said, sweeping her arm toward the table. "There's plenty." She leaned close to me. "Edgar's here," she whispered. "I told him you were coming."

"What did he say?" I said, trying to sound casual but wishing I had had a chance to brush my hair once I'd taken off my hat.

She smiled. "You know him. He blushed — that's all. And smiled. Doesn't he have the prettiest eyes?"

He does.

"Come on with me," Sarah said, taking my arm and tugging me toward the fireplace. She dropped her voice till it was low, almost a whisper. "Have you met Israel?" she said.

"Who?" I said.

I thought I said it but then realized that no sound had come out. I just turned and stared at her, feeling the blood leave my head, feeling light-headed, weak.

"Israel," Sarah said. She frowned at me. "I know you know about Israel. Don't you?"

"You know about him?" I said.

She laughed. "Everyone does. Well, not everyone. But everyone here, four families. Four Quaker families. He's right over there. Usually the underground passes us right by, goes right up to Boston. But the bad storms have made the ships stop here awhile. That's why Israel's still here."

I looked where she pointed. Sitting in a small chair by the fireplace, almost hidden by a corner of the fireplace and the huge spit, was the man Israel, his dark head bent. He was listening to someone, nodding at someone, deep in conversation.

I had not seen him in the light before, and I was surprised at how small he was, bent over even as he sat. He had been crouched when I'd seen him before, but even so, he'd seemed bigger.

But sitting right there? Out in the open?

"What if someone saw him?" I said. "Why isn't he hiding?"

"On Christmas Eve?" said a voice from behind me.

I turned to see Brother Foster standing there, smiling down at me. "On Christmas Eve," he said, "there should be no hunters, no hunted."

No.

He smiled at me. "Thou should go talk to Israel," he said. "Thou and he have met only under extreme circumstances. When the wolves are at the door, the bounty hunters, we keep him where it's safest."

"But what if somebody sees him now? And tells?"

"Who would tell?" Brother Foster asked.

Me. A hundred dollars.

"Besides," Brother Foster said quietly, "even now there's a plan. I have three sons outside, caring for the horses. And watching the house. Israel could be gone in a moment."

"Oh," I said.

"And tell what?" he went on, a quizzical, smiling look on his face. "Tell that there is a slave here? There is no slave here."

I looked over at Israel, then back at Brother Foster.

"There is no slave here," he repeated quietly. "For no man can be a slave."

⌒ Chapter Fifteen ⌒

Sarah led and I followed, across the room to where Israel was sitting, alone now, a plate of food balanced on his lap.

"Israel," Sarah said, turning to me and tugging me forward, "this is my friend, Gen — Genevieve."

Israel looked up. He smiled at me, showing even white teeth, and I was surprised to see he was younger than I'd thought. "How do you do, Miss Genevieve?" he said softly. "We meet under kinder conditions."

He held out a hand. "Forgive me for not rising to greet you," he went on. "I sit so much better than I stand."

I took his hand — the first time I had held a hand like his.

He held on to mine for a moment.

"Israel had to be in a coffin for four whole days!" Sarah said. "He was cramped up, and he hasn't been able to walk right since then. But Papa says he'll get better soon."

"A coffin?" I said, pulling my hand out of his. I suddenly had this terrifying picture in my head of him dead, then come back to life.

Israel nodded. "It's how I got here," he said. "In a coffin. My rescuers call it a ghost ship. Shipped up the coast in a coffin. It's rather safe that way." He laughed then. "Most folks don't want to open and inspect a coffin, don't you know?"

"I know I wouldn't!" Sarah said. "I —"

"Sarah! Sarah, child!"

It was Sarah's mother calling to her, and Sarah turned and hurried away. "I'll be back," she said over her shoulder to me.

"Will you sit?" Israel said to me, motioning to the hearth bench beside him.

I didn't want to, felt awkward, strange, but since I didn't know what else to do, I sat.

There was silence while I struggled to find something to say, but Israel spoke first. "Not many young women take on work the way you do," he said. "I've heard much about you."

I looked down at my hands in my lap. "It's not much, really," I answered. "I just do what I have to do — that's all."

He laughed a little. "Don't we all?" he said. "Don't we all? But you have courage. That's special."

I shook my head. "That's what Mrs. Foster just said, but I don't think so." I looked at him then, twisted and bent the way he was. "I think you must have courage, though," I said. "Closed up in a coffin!"

He sighed. "I thought so once," he said. "Don't anymore."

"Why?" I asked.

He looked down at his plate, at his hands suddenly clutching it so tightly it was shaking. He set the plate down on the floor beside him, then folded his arms and tucked his trembling hands into his armpits. "Because I ran away," he said quietly. "Because I couldn't stand to watch my wife and little boy being beaten. The master there, he whipped the women and children like a savage. Not the men, for some reason, not as fearsome anyway. He made us watch, and I couldn't bear that. So I ran."

"Watch?" I said.

I was about to say, Why didn't you make him stop? But I realized.

"I vowed to send for them," Israel went on. "Soon as I got North, I vowed I'd do it, soon as I got money. Then winter came on so bad." He shook his head and looked around the room. "I can't even make my way on to Canada, not even with the help of all these folks here. Not yet, anyway."

I didn't know what to say. I had heard such stories. But was it true? He wasn't just making it up?

Israel sighed. "My son, Samuel," he went on. "He's only three years old. He doesn't even really understand what slavery's all about. But he's learning. You remember being three years old?"

His eyes were suddenly intent on mine.

"Yes," I said.

"What?" he asked. "Tell me. What do three-year-olds remember?"

"Oh, I remember my papa," I said, and I couldn't help smiling at the memory. "He used to carry me on his shoulders. It's the thing I remember most. He'd carry me down to the docks, to meet the sailors and to see to things on the ship. People said I was his little sailor girl."

"I wonder if Samuel will remember," Israel said, looking into the flames of the fire. "It may be an awful long time before I see him again. Never, if they sell him away."

"Oh, he'll remember!" I said quickly, wanting to reassure him, wanting him not to think what he was thinking. "He'll remember. He'd never forget his papa. I've never forgotten mine."

"He's gone, your papa?"

I looked into the fire, too. "Dead — lost at sea — I think. Everybody thinks. But not my sister."

"Some people never give up hoping," Israel said.

"Isn't that the strangest thing? Some of us do, and some of us don't."

I nodded. It was strange. And suddenly I hoped fiercely that Samuel would never give up hoping, never give up hoping for his papa to return.

"How come the Lord makes it so hard sometimes? I wonder," Israel went on quietly, as though talking more to himself than to me. "Those days, lying in that dark old coffin, I was feeling mighty sorry for myself. But then I remembered the good Lord, and you know something? He didn't have it so easy Himself!"

He laughed then, a deep chuckle.

I looked up and frowned at him. "Are you a preacher?" I asked. And then, because I thought that sounded somewhat rude, I added, "I mean, you talk like a preacher."

He nodded. "I am. Although we weren't allowed Bibles down Mississippi way, where I come from. Weren't allowed to learn to read them, neither."

"Not allowed to read?" I said. "Why?"

He shook his head a little, the way Mr. Hathaway does when he's feeling impatient with a slow student. "Knowledge can be a dangerous thing," he said, "when you're trying to keep a man a slave. But God won't let them keep us down for long. God will provide."

"That's what my mama says all the time," I said. "But I don't believe it."

"You don't?" He sounded surprised.

"No," I said. "I don't. God helps those who help themselves, maybe. But that's all."

He seemed to be considering that. "Well," he said. "I believe He works through us. And you're the best proof of that there is. Don't you think so?"

I shook my head no.

"Why, Miss Genevieve!" he said, leaning forward to me. "Brother Foster moves me on to Canada. All these fine folks in this room, they help each other and me. You help your family. You helped Simon Joe."

I frowned at him.

"Yes, I know," he said. "Word gets around. And you don't think that's God working through us? God's here in us when we help one another."

But we still have to do it. We're still on our own, aren't we?

"And," Israel said softly, "I pray each day that God's found some good folks to help my Rebecca and my Samuel. I surely hope He has. They could get the bad end of the stick because I ran away."

I turned and looked into the fire again, trying to picture what Israel must be picturing. His wife, his little Samuel, beaten by a master who could do anything he wanted with them — even sell them! And Israel, not free to help them, not even free to leave, to walk away. No food, closed up in a coffin.

We had had no food for a while. But I just went out and earned it.

Israel couldn't even do that, could he?

And where was God to help him?

"I think," Israel said softly, as though he were hearing my thoughts, "if God is anywhere, it's in people. I know He lives in Brother Foster. I know that."

I looked up then, at Israel's dark, deep-set eyes looking back at mine, looked across the room to Brother Foster, and the strangest thought crept into my head. Maybe, I thought, maybe Israel's right. Maybe God does live in people, some people, anyway. Brother Foster, he gave me a job. He paid me a lot of money for very little work. He trusted me.

Or maybe God came in the form of Leila, Leila who said, Don't do anything bad, anything evil. . . .

I could feel the pain like a lump in my throat. "I was going to turn you in," I whispered.

"I know," he said.

"You did not know!" I said.

He smiled. "I did. I saw it in your eyes. Why not? It's a fair amount of money. In your shoes, I'd think about it myself."

"But you wouldn't do it!" I said.

Israel smiled then, a small smile, but one that touched his eyes. He reached out as if to touch me but then drew back his hand. "Neither did you," he said softly. "Neither did you."

✑ Chapter Sixteen ✑

On Christmas morning, I woke early, the sky barely light, just streaks of paler greenish blue beginning to show above the horizon.

I slid out of bed, built up the fire, then tiptoed down the hall to Mama's room and went in. She was sleeping quietly, her hair spread out on the pillow around her, her mouth slightly open. She looked perfectly normal in her sleep, and I prayed that she'd feel more like herself for Christmas Day.

I quietly fixed her fire, too, then laid out some clothes for her, thinking it might help her, not to have to make even that decision. When I finished that, I went on down the stairs to build up the fires in the sitting room and kitchen. When the kitchen fire was hot, I put on the kettle, then went and stood by the window, looking across the frozen snow to Sarah's house.

There was a candle flickering in each of the windows downstairs, and I pictured Sarah inside, finding Christmas treats, helping set the huge table for the family meal, her little nephews squabbling and playing, trying out their Christmas toys.

I thought then about Israel, where he was that day, tried to picture his wife, Rebecca, his son, Samuel, down South where they say it's warm even on Christmas Day, where some kinds of people own other kinds of people, where those other kinds of people can't work for money and can't learn to read. But I couldn't picture it, not at all.

I turned back from the window and went to the front parlor.

As I crossed the front hall, I heard Leila above me, looked up, and saw her running down the stairs.

"Merry Christmas!" she said, throwing her arms out wide. "Today's the day."

"Merry Christmas!" I said back, and I pulled her to me and hugged her hard.

My sister, I thought. No one will sell you away.

I held her like that for a long minute, hugging her to me, until she began to squirm. She looked up at me, laughing. "You're being very squeezy today," she said.

"It's because I love you," I said.

She looked surprised. "I love you, too," she said quietly.

I realized how seldom I said that anymore, although I surely meant it.

"I wonder how Mama will be today," she said.

"Better," I said. "I hope she's better."

Leila frowned at me. "Now, don't get angry, all right?" she said.

"On Christmas Day?" I answered.

"All right," she said. "But I was thinking, do you think that even good news can be bad for somebody who's sick?"

I took a deep breath. "So you still think that letter is coming?" I said slowly.

She nodded. "Yes. Soon. Oh, Gen!" She clasped her hands in front of her. "I see it. I see it so clearly, it's —"

There were steps above us then, and we looked up to see Mama coming down the stairs. She was wearing the clothes I had laid out, but her hair was tangled and needed brushing, and she walked unsteadily, trailing one hand along the wall.

I hurried forward and took her arm when she got to the foot of the stairs. "Mama!" I said. "How do you feel?"

"Weak," she answered.

But she'd answered!

"I had the strangest dream," she said, looking from

one of us to the other, blinking, as though she were still seeing dream people, not the real us.

I led her gently toward the parlor. "Mama, tell us in the parlor, where it's warm," I said. "I've fixed the fire. It's freezing here in the hall."

"Today is Christmas Day, is it not?" Mama said.

I smiled at her. "Yes, it is, Mama. And wait till you see the present I have for you."

Tears suddenly glistened in Mama's eyes. "I don't have anything for you girls," she said, her voice barely a whisper.

"It's all right, Mama," I said.

"Don't worry, Mama," Leila said almost at the same time. "We don't need anything. Now, come! Let me help you get settled in your chair."

"Yes," Mama said, "you do that. And I'll tell you my dream."

I went back to the kitchen then and got the tea things and made some hot buttered toast. I brought it all to the parlor, setting it on a small table beside Mama, then poured Mama's tea, then some for Leila and some for me. Then, while Leila helped Mama to sugar and milk, I stood looking around us. We had no tree this year, but Leila and I had put some cut pine boughs around the mantel and filled a basket with pinecones. The room was warm and cheerful and smelled the way a room should smell at Christmastime.

We were all settled with our tea when Mama began to talk. "I dreamed of birds," she said. "Wild birds, circling round and round our house."

I looked at Leila and she at me.

"One of the birds," Mama went on, staring down into her tea, "was strange. It frightened me."

"Mama!" Leila interrupted, her voice so broken, so terrified-sounding that I turned to her in alarm.

But Leila wasn't looking at me, nor was she looking at Mama. She was looking beyond Mama, out the window to the street — the street where a carriage had pulled up, where the coachman was handing someone down.

I looked at the clock on the mantel. Seven-thirty. Who would come calling at seven-thirty on Christmas morning?

Leila grasped my hand. "Open the door. Go! Do it!" she whispered.

The letter? No post would come on Christmas Day.

But I put down my teacup, got up, hurried down the hall to the front, and opened the door even before there was a knock.

Mrs. Morgan stood there, Captain Morgan's wife, her wide body filling the doorway, her fancy hat trembling with feathers and fake cherries.

"Merry Christmas, Genevieve," she said. "Forgive me for calling so early. Is your mama at home?"

For one ridiculous moment, I thought, And where else would she be? But I only said, "Yes. Yes, she's in the parlor. Please come in."

I held the door wide for her as she came in. "May I take your coat?" I asked.

"I'm not staying long," she answered. "There's church soon. But this was urgent."

Urgent.

"Please come," I said, and I led the way down the hall, Mrs. Morgan's footsteps thumping behind me on the bare wood floor, my heart thumping hard in my throat.

I opened the door to the parlor, and Mrs. Morgan swept in, crossed the room to Mama, then bent and placed a kiss somewhere near Mama's cheek. "Merry Christmas, Ann," she said. She pulled back and frowned at Mama. "I must say you don't look very well."

"Mama's been a little sick," I said.

Mrs. Morgan turned to me. "I need to speak to your mama alone," she said.

Leila quickly stood up to go, but I took her hand and pulled her to me. "No," I said. "Whatever you have to say, you can say it to all of us together."

Mrs. Morgan's eyebrows went up, and she turned to Mama. "Well, my word!" she said.

"Let them stay," Mama whispered. "They're good girls."

Mrs. Morgan let out a deep huffy breath, like a horse. "Well," she said. "I'm glad my girls aren't so uppity. Captain Morgan would never allow it."

She glared at Leila and me while a long moment passed.

I don't care about Captain Morgan! I don't care what he'd allow! I want to know why you're here! Those words didn't come out, though, and my throat ached with tension.

Mrs. Morgan made another of those huffy horse breaths, then dug deep into her reticule and took out a folded sheet of paper and an envelope. She held them out toward Mama. "These arrived just last night on the cargo ship that picks up mail," she said. "It was too late to call on you, so I brought them round first thing this morning."

Her hand was outstretched to Mama, but Mama had closed her eyes and was shaking her head hard back and forth.

I crossed the room to Mama. "It's all right, Mama," I whispered. I put a hand on her hair, patted it gently. I held out my other hand toward Mrs. Morgan. "You can give them to me," I said.

She did, putting a folded paper and an envelope in my hand, a fat envelope.

I looked down at it. It was addressed to Mama and Leila and me — in Papa's hand.

I looked up at Mrs. Morgan, trying to see what was in her face, hardly daring to hope. A new letter? Or one just arrived from years ago?

"He's all right, your papa," Mrs. Morgan said gently, her voice kinder than I'd ever heard it before. "He's on Captain Morgan's ship, and he's fine."

Tears sprang to my eyes, and I looked at Leila, and she looked at me, and then we both turned to Mama. Tears were streaming down our faces, all of us — Mama's, too, although her eyes were still shut and she was still shaking her head back and forth, back and forth.

"That letter, that page," Mrs. Morgan went on, and I thought there were tears in her eyes, too, "is from Captain Morgan to me, explaining all that happened. You may read that, too. I'll leave it with you. The other, the envelope, was addressed to you, and of course I didn't open it. And now you have it."

I could feel Leila trembling, pressed against my side. "Is he really all right?" she whispered. "Are you sure he's all right?"

"Quite all right," Mrs. Morgan said. "I'm sure he'll tell you so in his own letter. In fact, according to Captain Morgan, he's in remarkably good health considering what he's been through."

Mama opened her eyes then. "Been through?" she whispered.

"Yes, lost his ship and almost all his men," Mrs. Morgan said. "I'd say he's been through something."

"Lost his ship?" Mama cried. She leaned forward in her chair, her eyes wide. "He's lost his ship?"

Mrs. Morgan frowned. "Yes, I'm sorry to tell you, but it's true. He was trapped by an early winter storm, and his ship was crushed by the ice. But he was able to make it to land, he and a few of his men. They've been living with the Inuit. Savages, it seems to me, but I guess they cared for him well enough. Captain Morgan was able to get in there during the warm months. He's bringing them home, but it will be some time yet, summer probably, before they reach home."

"Oh, but their wives!" Mama cried. "How will they go on?"

"They will, Mama," I said softly. "They will. Don't worry yourself."

Suddenly I couldn't wait for Mrs. Morgan to leave, leave so we could read the letter, leave so we could talk, just us. I wanted to hug Leila and Mama and have us tell each other over and over: Papa's coming home! Papa's coming home.

Papa was coming home to us.

⌒ Chapter Seventeen ⌒

I read the letter aloud after Mrs. Morgan had gone, as Mama asked me to. I was trembling so much that I had to sit with it, and even then my hand shook so that the letter trembled as though in a breeze. Mama was shaking, too, pressing her hands hard together.

Beside me, Leila sat, leaning forward, reading along.

I took a deep breath and began:

" 'My Beloved Family,

" 'I am writing one letter to all of you since there is so much to say and saying it three times would be too hard for me. It is painful to recall certain things, and it has also been a long time since I have held a pen in hand, a long time since I have seen anything so civilized as a pen and paper.

" 'By now, I hope, you will have heard or read of our great loss, and I will not dwell on all the details

now but will tell you more when we are at last together. Suffice it to say, we were caught in a winter
storm — in early August two years ago it was, the
worst storm I have seen in all my years at sea. We did
everything to save ourselves, but in vain. We faced it,
fought it, tied everything down, tried every which way
to save ourselves. Some men even tied themselves to
the masts to keep from being blown away, but then
the masts broke loose and were torn off and the men
with them. Waves froze right over us as soon as they
struck, and a devil's wind blew and the ice ripped the
keel — and finally, after two days and a night of this,
the storm blew itself out. But by then the ship was
lost and every man aboard with it but for myself and
two mates, one of whom later died. I do not know
to this day why God preserved our lives and not the
others', but it is something I will spend my life considering and praying over and trying to be worthy of.

" 'We were rescued in the oddest way — first by
the birds. There was a flock of them, five or six, and
one in particular flew round and round over our heads
on the first day that the storm was gone, as we clung
to what little bit remained of the ship. We did not recognize the birds, although we were sure they were
land birds since we know all the seabirds. So we tried
something that easily could have cost us our lives —
but what did we have to lose? We would surely die

in the frozen waters in a few hours anyway. So we tore loose a bit of planking from the ship, made ourselves a crude raft, rigged a sail, and set out, following the birds.

" 'In a few hours, when we were beginning to be sure that we would freeze to death, suddenly, out of the mist appeared a small dugout with two Eskimos — Inuit — who took us home with them to their village.

" 'The rest is a long, long story of the mercy of God and man's kindness to man. I will tell you much about it in the years to come. But in short, for two years, one month, and six days we lived with those Inuit — I marked the days off with a small stick on a piece of wood that somehow had been saved — sharing their every day, every meal, their fires and dogs and warm clothes. They fed us, clothed us, taught us their ways, and in turn, we did what we could to be of use to them. I have learned to hunt, to fish through the ice, to follow the tribe to summer quarters, to listen for the sound of the walrus, a staple of our diet for those years, to understand the prayer to the soul of the walrus. And I will tell you more, much more, about their worship and their gods, when I am with you.

" 'But for now, what I really want to say is this: I have missed you more than I could ever imagine these long years. There is nothing so precious to a man as his family, those he loves. How does anyone live without others to love? My heart ached, missing you. I lived over and over again in memory every detail of our home life, my walks with you all on summer nights, looking up at the stars, our warm hearth in the winter, our stories at night. My dear wife, how I missed your warmth, your love. Ann, Leila, Gen, I ached — and still do — to feel your arms. Sometimes, at night, I would see you so clearly in my dreams, and I would wake, happy, my heart beating fast, sure that you were there. And I am not ashamed to say that I cried real tears for you — and for myself — when I realized you were not.

" 'And then, my dear ones, how I've worried about you! I knew to a cent how much money you had, how much we had saved, how it was planned for expenses, food, heat, clothing, spread over a year to two. But then, as one year stretched into two, as the days and seasons turned to three, I knew your resources had run out. And although I know how frugal and smart you are, I knew — know — that lately you have been poor indeed. My dear Genevieve, I know so much must have fallen on your shoulders over these years. And my Leila, my little bird, how has my dreamer survived these harsh years? I have worried over each of you and how you were surviving this change in fortune. I pray for you even now, ache for you, want to do for you. But how can I?

" 'I have no idea how you have managed, but I believe you have, and I pray to God you have, have taken in boarders, accepted help, done something. I feel near to a failure for letting you down, yet I believe you have managed somehow. And somehow, I am going to make it all up to you. It will be hard at first — a sea captain without a ship — but thank God, I am able-bodied still, and we will survive.

" 'I must admit that there were times that I thought I would never see you again. How hard those days were, days when I almost gave up hope. But now again, I hope. I believe. I will see you soon. It may be many months yet. Captain Morgan has a job to do, ports to be visited, and I am simply his passenger. How blessed we are that he chanced to pass so far north into the Arctic, on the track of a whale, or he'd never have seen our shipwreck, never have seen us waving to him from shore. But we are on our way now. We will be home by early summer, we believe. And I will hold you close in my arms again.

" 'For now, my dearly loved ones, I hold you in my heart. And love you more than I can ever say.

" 'And with this letter, I can truly say: All is well.

" 'Your devoted husband.

" 'Your adoring papa.' "

☙ Chapter Eighteen ☜

The week between Christmas and the New Year sped by, and it was finally New Year's Night, the night of the recital. It had been a wonderful week, filled with so many delights. The most wonderful of course was that all we thought about, Leila and me, all we talked about, was Papa. At last! Papa.

How delightful not to worry. How exciting to look forward. And how right Leila had been to hold on to hope. How had she known? But even though I asked her, she didn't know. And she said she especially didn't understand about the birds that led Papa to land, or how that matched her dream of being a falcon.

It didn't matter, though. All that mattered was that Papa was safe, safe and coming home to us — although I had to read his letter over and over again to really believe it, and Leila and Mama did, too.

Mama was still odd, although not nearly so silent as earlier, and she seldom cried anymore. Sometimes she even laughed, especially when we talked together at dinnertime.

There was one other thing that happened that week that was important. That cart was outside the store again one day, loaded with lumber and shingles, and when I went in, Brother Foster and his sons were there again, warming themselves by the fire, all red-faced with cold, the cold air seeming to rise right off their clothing. They'd been to a barn raising, and the material in the cart was left over, Brother Foster said, and could they possibly . . . ?

Yes! I said. Although I didn't dare look at them.

But by the next day, we had a new roof and the broken-out window had been repaired, and already the house felt warmer.

Now it was finally New Year's Night, and Leila and I were going to the recital. Best of all, Edgar's papa had said he could go, too. We dressed as warmly as we could and headed for the town hall, where the recital was to be. Sarah's papa had offered to take us in his horse and buggy, but we wanted to be together, to walk alone in the dark. Mama still wouldn't leave the house, shook her head violently at the suggestion, but she did wave to us from the parlor window.

It was freezing cold on our walk, the coldest weather

we'd had, and we walked closely, arm in arm. The snow crunched under our feet, and overhead the sky was black and dotted with stars.

Leila kept tripping, and I had to keep catching her arm, because she wasn't looking where she was going, was walking head tilted back, looking up at the sky.

"Will you pay attention!" I said after I had caught her for about the tenth time.

"I'm looking for falling stars," she said.

"Well, you're going to fall yourself," I said.

"Will not," she answered.

"Will, too," I said. "And besides, why do you want to see a falling star? There's nothing left to wish for, is there?"

Leila laughed up at me. "Of course there is! There's always something left to wish for."

"Like what?" I said. "Now that Papa's coming home, what else could you possibly wish for?"

"That I don't forget my lines tonight. That I don't trip going up on the stage. That Imogene is there. That I get a pony!" she said.

"A pony?" I said, turning to stare at her.

She nodded, very matter-of-fact. "I want a pony."

I just laughed, but I thought it was really a wonderful wish, a wonderful, foolish wish!

"Where would you put a pony?" I said.

She shrugged. "In the backyard. When Papa comes home, he'll get one for me."

"I hope so, Leila," I said. "I hope so."

We were at the town hall then, and Leila clutched my arm extra hard as we went up the steps. "I'm scared," she whispered.

"You're going to do fine. You've been rehearsing all day."

"But what if I forget my lines?" she said.

I just laughed.

Inside, the hall was crowded with people — parents and aunts and uncles and cousins — all dressed in their Sunday best, and suddenly I felt scared, too. Up till then, I'd been only a little worried about my part, but mostly just excited. Now, though, it was just so . . . imposing in there!

In the back of the room, a small chamber ensemble was setting up its instruments, and in the front, two flags were hanging by the stage, the American flag and the flag of Massachusetts. All this for us, so people could listen to us?

What if I stumbled or forgot my lines?

Silly. You sound just like Leila.

I searched the crowd for Sarah, saw her waving to me from across the room, and made my way to her through the crowd.

Leila had run ahead, abandoned me as soon as she

saw her friend Imogene. They were standing onstage now, swinging hands, and she didn't look the least bit nervous in spite of what she'd said.

Sarah took my arm as we went up the stage steps to where Mr. Hathaway was pacing back and forth, consulting some kind of list. "I'm so scared, I'm going to faint!" she whispered.

"You?" I whispered back. "Me!"

Mr. Hathaway turned to us then, his face and neck even pinker than usual. He grabbed our arms and pushed us roughly down into seats in the front row. "You're late!" he said. "Both of you. Now, get settled!"

I just looked at Sarah, and she shrugged. We weren't late, but I think we both understood — he was as nervous as we were.

We had just taken our seats when Sarah leaned close and whispered, "Look who's coming!"

I looked. Edgar, coming up the stage steps.

"Over here!" Mr. Hathaway said to him, and he took Edgar by the arm, as roughly as he had done to us, and pushed him down into the seat next to me.

Next to me!

I had never sat next to a boy before. At school, boys sit on one side, girls on the other. At church, too. Even at Brother Foster's house at the party that night, I had sat across the table from Edgar.

I thought of what Sarah and I had just said about fainting. What if I *did* faint? Then what?

Edgar would have to pick me up off the floor.

I thought of those romantic novels I sometimes sneak out of Mama's room, of heroines fainting, being carried off by their beaus. In Mama's novels, there are always beaus.

I snuck a sideways look at him.

His ears were red — well, the one I could see was red. Was it from the cold? Or was he embarrassed, just as I was?

"Say something to him," Sarah whispered. "Good evening or something."

"Can't!" I whispered back.

"You're being a dolt!" she said.

The violins began tuning up, and suddenly the whole room quieted. All the buzzing, talking, humming sounds of people, the scraping of chairs — all was stilled.

For a few minutes, the ensemble tuned up. And then finally they struck up the notes for the hymn, "Amazing Grace," and everyone stood up, even those of us on the stage.

After we sang, Reverend Toomies from the Congregational church said the blessing, and we all sat down. Then Mr. Hathaway stood up.

"This evening," Mr. Hathaway said, and his voice

came out a bit trembly, "is a chance for these young people to show what they've learned. It's also an opportunity for all together to welcome the New Year."

And then he introduced Emma Badger as the first speaker, Emma who was younger even than Leila, and he sat down.

I snuck a look at Sarah, wondering if she was thinking what I was thinking: that never have I heard Mr. Hathaway be so brief. But Sarah was just leaning forward, listening to Emma.

Emma said a small Mother Goose rhyme that was very sweet, and then the twins Fannie and Jewel Martin got up and said one about the woods on a summer day, and everyone laughed, and then it was Leila's turn. I had heard her say her piece many times in the last few weeks, but I kept sending her good thoughts, praying that she wouldn't forget even a single word.

She went right to the edge of the stage in front of me, standing straight and tall. Her thin cotton dress barely covered the back of her knees, and I wished I had somehow found a way to get her a new dress or at least to remake one of mine.

She paused and clasped her hands together, then spoke in this small, clear voice that could take your breath away. Her poem was a Christmas poem, about what Santa could bring, what little girls hoped for and little boys wished for, what babies dreamed of on Christmas Day.

It was a simple poem, but it was the way she said it that was so special. Her voice was clear and sweet, direct and personal, as though she were talking to each single person — you and you and you.

There was a lot of applause when she was finished, and I clapped especially hard.

Then it was Edgar's turn.

His was a patriotic poem, about the importance of the flag, but he was shaking so, that even his voice shook. I wanted to tell him to slow down and take deep breaths, even found myself taking them for him, but I guess he didn't get my message.

He raced through it, his voice quavering, and once he forgot a line, and Mr. Hathaway prompted him.

When he finished and turned back to his seat, his face was so pale, I thought he'd faint!

The applause for him was just polite. Before I could think too much or change my mind, I quick leaned over and whispered to him. "You did just fine!"

And then it was our turn, Sarah's and mine.

We had prepared the reading in two parts, as though one were speaking and one were answering, softly, almost like an echo, because it is the kind of reading that lends itself to that.

We went to the front of the stage and stood side

by side, looking out at the audience. I looked for a familiar face, knowing Mama wasn't there, and saw Brother Foster, saw him smiling at me, and for some reason, I remembered what Israel had said about him.

I took a deep breath, concentrated on keeping my voice pitched low, and said the first line. " 'My soul doth magnify the Lord,' " I said.

And for the first time in a very long time, I suddenly realized I meant the words — I believed them. My soul did magnify the Lord, did swell to meet Him, did rejoice in His coming. At least tonight it did.

" 'And my spirit hath rejoiced in God my Savior,' " Sarah was answering softly. " 'Because He hath regarded the humility of His handmaid.' "

It was my turn then, and then her turn, my line, then her line:

" 'For behold, from henceforth, all generations shall call me blessed. For He that is mighty hath done great things for me, and holy is His name. And His mercy shall be from generation unto generation, unto them that fear Him. For He hath shown might with His arm; He hath scattered the proud in the conceit of their hearts. He hath put down the mighty from their seats, and hath exalted the humble. He hath filled the hungry with good things, and the rich He hath sent empty away. He hath given help to Israel, His servant, mindful of his mercy. Even as He spoke to our fathers, to Abraham, and to his seed forever.' "

There was no applause after we finished and sat down, not a sound, only silence. Only Edgar turned to me, a smile on his face, and I felt my face get scarlet as I smiled back at him.

And then there was a shuffling sound, soft at first, then louder, and people in the audience were pushing back their chairs and standing. Then, like a great murmuring chorus, one, and then another, and then another, they said, "Amen."

⋐ Chapter Nineteen ⋑

Months went by, and spring came, and still we waited for Papa to return. I often went down to the sea, stood looking out across the water to the horizon, feeling something inside me that I couldn't identify. I knew only that it was a huge feeling, as if something were swelling in my heart. Papa was out there. And one day this very ocean would carry him home to me.

Mama must have been feeling something new and happy, too, although she did not talk about it. Yet I could tell. She still sat by the window, staring out, but she didn't spend nearly as much time there as she once had. Now I sometimes found her in front of the looking glass in her room, trying new ways to fix her hair, rubbing her cheeks with her fingers to bring color there. And one day she took all the clothes from her wardrobe and mended them, adding bits of lace and trimmings. She would be happy, and better, too, when Papa came home, I knew.

And Leila — Leila was almost beside herself with the excitement of waiting, was like a little spirit, flitting here and there, so excited some days she would skip all the way to school, her arms outstretched on either side, tilting side to side like a little bird. She no longer listened on the stairs at night — at least, she said she didn't — but still, I would wake some nights just as she was slipping back into bed beside me. When I asked where she'd been, though, she'd just say she had gotten up to use the chamber pot or else to get her angel doll. I didn't believe her, but I also knew she wouldn't tell me till she was ready to tell.

And so we waited, each in our own way.

It was a quiet, breezy night in late spring, one of those soft nights that gives promise that summer will really come, when I woke to find Leila gone from the bed beside me. I sat up and looked around. She wasn't in the room, and her dressing gown was missing from the foot of the bed.

I got up, pulled my dressing gown on, and tiptoed down the hall toward the stairs, sure she'd be down there, listening.

When I got out into the hallway, I felt a cold wind blowing, a draft as though a door were ajar. Had I forgotten to close up, forgotten to close the downstairs door?

I started down the stairs but realized the wind was coming from behind me, from upstairs.

I turned and saw it then — saw the door to the attic. It was standing ajar, a breeze blowing it gently to and fro.

Leila! Was she up there? Had she gone up the attic stairs, and then outside onto the roof walkway?

Foolish Leila! No one had been out on that walkway in years, not since Mama had stopped looking from there, anyway. The walkway probably wasn't even safe anymore, the floorboards rotted, the railings rusted!

I hurried up the narrow attic stairs, pulling my dressing gown about me, lifting it so I could see the steps.

Once I was in the attic, I could see the door to the outside — see that it stood open.

I shook my head, then went to the door and stepped out onto the narrow walkway, out into the night air.

Leila was there, her back to me, her face turned up to the sky. The wind whipped her hair about her, blew her dressing gown back and forth, twisting it around her feet. The moonlight lay on her hair, making it shine, a halo of light and wind-whipped hair. She turned to me then, as though she knew I was there, although I knew I hadn't made a sound.

"Oh, Genevieve!" she said. "Look!"

She held up her arms, as though embracing the sky, then dropped them, a sheepish smile on her face. She stretched one hand out to me then, reaching for my hand.

I should have scolded her for being up there, for endangering herself, for not being in bed asleep. Instead I went to her and took her hand in mine.

We stood side by side for a time, silently looking around us. What a wild, glorious view of the town, the harbor, the ships seen from so high, the ocean stretching off to the horizon as far as I could see. Many masts were visible out there, ships that tied up just off-shore to await a tow, others that simply waited for daylight before docking. Above and around us, the sky was a canopy of stars reaching right down to the sea, the stars reflecting and winking back at themselves from the black water, creating a double sky.

"Papa's sky!" Leila whispered.

Yes, Papa's sky.

"Maybe he's looking at it right now," Leila went on softly. "Maybe right this minute, he's looking at these very same stars."

I nodded. "I think that about Papa often," I said.

And then for some reason, I thought of Israel and of his wife and child. Were they looking at the sky and thinking of each other? Were they as blessed as we were? Would they ever be reunited?

I must have sighed, because Leila said, "What?"

"Nothing," I said. "I was just thinking. I wish everyone could be as blessed as we are."

"I know," Leila said. "I know."

Suddenly I felt her hand tighten in mine, and she began to tremble.

"Come on!" I said. "You're going back to bed. You're shivering."

She shook her head violently, grasping my hand hard and holding it tightly with both of her own. "Wait!" she said. "Wait just one more minute."

"You're getting a chill," I said.

"Look!" It was almost triumphant the way she said it. "On the horizon! Way out! It's a ship. Way far out to the horizon!"

I looked where she was looking, but at first all I could see on the horizon was a dot. But then, as I watched, it suddenly began to change, became a ship, a huge, many-masted ship. It seemed to grow quickly, coming closer and closer, riding high on the waves, gently lifting, falling, lifting again, the moon lighting its billowing sails.

I hadn't seen a ship this huge in a long time.

Papa — on Captain Morgan's ship?

I looked at Leila and she at me. And then, strange — I heard something, something I could not be hearing, and yet I was hearing it. I was! I heard a voice I could not be hearing.

"Leila?" I said.

She smiled. Smiled and turned to me, her head to one side, that way she has of listening. And I knew then that she was hearing it, too, the voice we could not be hearing.

"All is well," the voice said.

All is well.